"You mean everything to me. I love you."

She shook her head. "You don't love me, not really. I'm nothing more than a responsibility to you."

"Don't tell me how I feel." Desperation turned to anger in a flash. Cole jumped to his feet and began to pace. "I've been in love with you since I was sixteen years old, but you never saw me, not really. You only had eyes for Billy. It nearly killed me when you married him, but I stuffed down my anger and hurt and congratulated both of you, because really, what else could I do?"

"No, that can't be true."

"It's true, all right. I wish to God it wasn't. I tried to push away my feelings for you, tried to love other women, but none of them were you. None of them compared to you. I thought I'd get over you, but I never did."

Her eyes were wide with shock. "Cole—"

"Billy guessed the truth. I found out he'd been cheating on you, and I confronted him. We had a huge fight, beat each other till we were both bloody. He told me I was jealous because you'd rejected me. He said you'd never want me, that you'd always be tied to him, no matter what happened. And he was right." He gave a bark of mirthless laughter. "He's dead and he still comes between us."

Praise for Jana Richards

"Talented author Jana Richards, with her gift for creating snappy dialogue, honest, lovable characters—human and canine—has given us another winner. Do not miss *CHILL OUT*. You'll be as entranced as I was."

~Wild Woman Authors blog

~*~

"Where the hell has this author been and why haven't I read her before? This book is fantastic!"

~Christine K, The TBR Pile

~*~

"Richards has a knack of developing characters with real depth."

~Belinda Williams, Belinda Williams Books

~*~

"Ms. Richards knows how to keep a reader turning page after page."

~Coffee Time Romance

~*~

"So, in summary, put aside your book markers because you won't need them; turn off the phone because you won't want to be interrupted, lock the door, and ENJOY this one by Jana Richards."

~Seriously Reviewed

Child of Mine

by

Jana Richards

The Masonville Series, Book 1

This is a work of fiction. Names, characters, places, and incidents are either the product of the author's imagination or are used fictitiously, and any resemblance to actual persons living or dead, business establishments, events, or locales, is entirely coincidental.

Child of Mine

Contact Information: info@thewildrosepress.com

Cover Art by *Rae Monet, Inc. Design*

The Wild Rose Press, Inc.
PO Box 708
Adams Basin, NY 14410-0708
Visit us at www.thewildrosepress.com

Publishing History
First Champagne Rose Edition, 2019
Print ISBN 978-1-5092-2480-7
Digital ISBN 978-1-5092-2481-4

The Masonville Series, Book 1
Published in the United States of America

Chapter One

August 1

Lauren Walsh watched as her husband's coffin was lowered into the grave. The minister's voice sounded far away, as if she were trapped underwater. She struggled to keep from drowning.

"We commit the body of Billy Walsh to the earth: ashes to ashes, dust to dust. Into the smiles of our memories, we lay you down. May you rest in peace and love."

She closed her eyes and squeezed her sister's hand. *It'll be over soon. I can pretend for a few more minutes.*

"Billy lived his life to the fullest. And though he was taken too soon and his passing grieves us immensely, let's rejoice that he lived the life he wanted. Let's remember his spirit and his zest for life, and be happy we knew him."

Anger made her throat burn. They knew nothing about Billy. How could they? For the last five years she'd been lying to them. Lauren gulped deep, calming breaths. *It's almost over. Don't fall apart now.*

Following the lead of Billy's brother Cole, she tossed the white rose she held into the grave. *White roses for remembrance.* Memories swirled around her like ghosts. So many things she wished she could forget.

Beside her, Cole stood with his head bent, one arm around his weeping mother. Cole's pain was as raw as his mother's, and Lauren's heart ached for him. Whatever differences they'd had, Cole and Billy had been brothers, and blood was thicker than water. She reached for his free hand and squeezed it in silent support. Without looking at her, Cole returned the gesture.

"Lord, let now thy servant depart in peace, according to thy word."

The minister's words signaled the end of the interment ceremony. Lauren sighed with relief. With one last squeeze, Cole released her hand. Lauren looped her arm through her sister Charlotte's and hung on tight. She didn't know what she would have done without her older sister and the rest of her family these last few hellish days.

Ella Walsh sobbed uncontrollably as Cole led her to the waiting funeral car. She leaned against him, her cries piercing the quiet of the Masonville, North Dakota graveyard. "My Billy, my Billy. He can't be gone. No, no, no!"

Lauren wished she could feel grief. She'd been married to Billy for five years, had known him many years before that. Wasn't a wife who'd just lost her husband supposed to feel grief? But all she had was the guilt of their last conversation weighing on her heart and the anger that made her want to beat her fists against a wall.

The luncheon in the church basement, following the interment, dragged on with excruciating slowness. Lines of people stepped forward to offer their condolences. They were so sorry, they said. It was hard to believe someone as vital and alive as Billy could be dead, they said. They'd followed his hockey career since he was a star on the Masonville peewee team. He'd been on the verge of making the big leagues, they were sure. Such a tragedy that a car crash on a Georgia interstate had ended his life.

Lauren murmured her thanks, choking back screams of frustration. *Don't you know he was never going to make the National Hockey League?* There'd been a chance at one time; he'd had the talent, but not the work ethic. Or the right attitude. He'd been traded from one crummy minor league team to another. From one crummy minor league town to another. She'd worked at whatever job she could find to help support them. And even though it was obvious his hockey dream wouldn't come to fruition, Billy had stubbornly refused to deal with reality.

Finally the luncheon was over, and she and her family could leave. The oppressive August afternoon heat hit her as she stepped from the cool church basement. Anxious to escape, she followed her family to the car. On the short drive to her parents' acreage a few miles outside of Masonville, the car's air conditioner didn't have a chance to cool the interior, and a bead of sweat ran down her back beneath her long-sleeved knit dress, a dress too warm for this weather but the only black one she owned.

She was grateful for the coolness and peace of the house she'd grown up in. After kicking off her heels at the front door, she curled into a ball on the sofa in the living room. She closed her eyes, needing some quiet and peace to think. And time to figure out where she went from here.

What am I to do with my life now?

But the peace didn't last. The doorbell rang, shattering the quiet. Lauren heard her mother greet a couple of neighbors. She stifled a groan. She was expected to receive these guests and accept their condolences. After all, they were only doing what was considered the right thing by small town standards. She pushed to her feet and forced herself to walk to the kitchen.

Widowed elderly sisters Martha and Beatrice were longtime friends and neighbors of her parents, Grace and Robert Saunders. They greeted Lauren with sad, pitying smiles and two casserole dishes. Martha handed her dish to Lauren's mother.

"We didn't think you'd feel much like cooking today, Grace, so we brought some food." The smell of tuna fish casserole filled the kitchen. Martha turned to Lauren and grasped her hands. "We're so sorry for your loss, dear."

"Thank you." The words tasted like dust in her mouth.

"Billy was such a character," Beatrice said with a wistful shake of her head. "I had him in my grade two classroom. You were in the same class, Lauren. He was quite the little hell raiser. Remember, Martha?"

"Oh, yes, I remember. I had him for grade five. Nearly ripped all my hair out that year. Remember the time he pulled the fire alarm? We evacuated the school and called out the volunteer fire department before we realized it was one of Billy's pranks. I was spitting mad, but he was so angelic-looking, with that sweet smile of his, that I couldn't stay angry with him. He was curious to see what would happen, he said."

That was Billy in a nutshell. He'd do whatever he wanted to do, purely for fun, and would charm away any objections or anger. Lauren was often made to believe she was the one in the wrong, she was the one who was being unreasonable.

Her mother made tea and put a cup in front of her, but her stomach rebelled at the thought of drinking it. The old ladies went on and on about Billy until Lauren was sickened by all the memories. Instead of comforting her, they only succeeded in fueling her anger. Why had he done this to them? Why had he taken her love and thrown it in her face? And now he was dead, and she didn't even have the satisfaction of telling him how much he'd hurt her.

Sam Miller, one of Billy's childhood friends, swept into the kitchen, his face full of disbelief and anguish. He knelt beside her chair and gripped one of her clammy hands in his.

"I can't believe he's dead. I can't believe I'm not going to see him again. I'm so sorry, Lauren."

"Thank you," she said woodenly. They were the only words she was capable of uttering today.

"He was the best guy, a good friend, and a good husband. Nobody can replace him."

Lauren snatched her hand away and tucked it into her lap. Her jaw hurt from clenching it. Sam had no idea what kind of husband Billy had been. Like everyone else, he'd only seen the façade she'd created of the happy, doting wife to the charming, athletic husband. It had been easy to deceive everyone in Masonville. She and Billy lived most of the year in the southern cities of the minor hockey league he'd played in, only coming home for holidays and special occasions. She'd maintained the façade till the end, until Billy's last deceit. Even then, she couldn't tell the truth, not even to Charlotte, the person she trusted most in the world. She'd been too ashamed, too humiliated.

The doorbell rang again. Charlotte answered it, and a trio of neighbors came through the door, each carrying more food. The odor of greasy fried chicken assaulted Lauren's senses. The smell and the thought of eating made her want to throw up.

Panic swirled in her gut along with the nausea. She couldn't do this anymore. She couldn't listen to their stories and memories of a Billy they really didn't know.

She pushed away from the table with an abruptness that caused her chair to nearly topple backward, saved only by Sam grabbing it.

"I have to go. I'm sorry, I can't…I need…"

What do I need?

She had no idea. She had to get out of this kitchen before she flew into a million pieces. But everyone was staring at her as if she'd lost her mind.

"I'm sorry," she repeated, edging toward the door. One more step and she could reach the hook where the keys to her mother's ancient Honda Civic were hanging. "I need to go."

"I'll come with you," Charlotte said.

"No!" She forced herself to calm down, needing to dispel the worried look from her sister's face. "I mean, I need to be by myself for a while. I'm fine, Char, really I am. But I'm not good company right now. I have to go."

She didn't wait for Charlotte's reply. Sliding her feet into a pair of her mother's flip-flops, she grabbed the car keys and pushed open the screen door, breaking into a run once she'd cleared the back steps. As her foot hit the gas pedal, she let out a relieved sigh, feeling like she could breathe again.

Lauren sped down the highway with no real idea where she was headed. She rolled down her window, letting the hot prairie wind howl through the car. How she wished the wind could blow away her troubled thoughts. But nothing could help her. Guilt and anger were so tangled with love and betrayal that she didn't know what to feel or think.

How I could I love Billy and hate him at the same time?

She needed to say goodbye. That last time she'd spoken to Billy, only days before his death, she'd been so angry, so hurt. They'd argued, and she'd said things she now regretted. She didn't want those ugly words to be the last thing she said to him.

Lauren turned the car around and drove the short distance to the cemetery, parking the Civic behind some trees where it couldn't be seen from the main road. As she got out of the car, she was greeted with the sound of birds singing in the trees and the sweet smell of freshly cut hay in a nearby field. A sense of homecoming washed over her. She'd missed North Dakota so much these past five years.

Grasshoppers jumped in all directions as she walked past the silent headstones to the freshly dug mound of earth where Billy had been laid to rest. She stared at the grave, her head bowed.

"We really made a mess of things, didn't we?"

The only reply was the sound of the wind blowing through the trees. "We both made a lot of mistakes. I lost faith in your dream, and I got tired of the way we were living. But you hurt me, Billy. You cheated and lied, and you hurt me."

Her eyes filled with tears, and she held back a sob. "I was so angry with you. I'm still angry with you. But I never wanted you to die! Why did you have to go and die?"

She drew a deep, shaky breath. "The last time I saw you, we fought and I said some horrible, ugly things to you. I'm sorry for that, Billy. I truly am. But you said some ugly things, too. Maybe someday I'll be able to forgive you for the things you've done, but I'm not sure I'll ever forget."

She stood silent over the grave for a long time. Finally, she looked up and saw the sun hanging low in the western sky. Her family would be worried about her. She wasn't ready to go home yet, but it was time to leave this place. Time to say goodbye.

"Goodbye Billy. I did love you. Once."

As she got back in the Civic and drove away from the cemetery, her emotions swirled in turmoil. Would she ever feel peace again?

Almost without realizing it, Lauren found herself on a back road that led to the secret spot in the pasture that Billy and Cole's father had once owned. The three of them had hung out there as teenagers, and she'd had her first, and only, cigarette there. She laughed out loud at the memory of the coughing fit that had followed her attempt at being cool. She remembered Billy's laughter and the way Cole had pounded her back to help her breathe.

She pulled up to the barbed-wire fence leading to the pasture. Cole's half-ton truck, easily identified by the logo of his veterinary clinic painted on the doors, was parked nearby. She wondered if he was struggling with memories, too.

She eased herself between two rows of barbed wire and followed a well-worn path to the hideout. Perhaps this place wasn't as secret as she'd once believed.

Cole sat on a log, staring into the cold ashes of a recent fire. He wore the same white dress shirt he'd worn to the funeral, his suit jacket lying on the ground next to him. He looked up in surprise as she approached.

"What are you doing here?" he asked.

"Running away." She sat on the log next to his. "I couldn't handle the casserole brigade."

"The what?"

"The endless train of people dropping by with food." She involuntarily shivered. "I can't face all the well-meaning platitudes and condolences right now."

He dipped his head in a nod. "That's the reason I left Mom's apartment. I couldn't take it anymore either."

She was glad he understood. "It looks like this place has been discovered. I guess it's not our little secret anymore."

Cole chuckled and pointed to his left, toward a clump of trees. An old couch had been dragged between the bushes. Beer cans were strewn nearby.

"Apparently not. Tim says kids come out here for bush parties almost every weekend, at least until the weather turns cold. He doesn't mind as long as they stay in this one corner of the pasture and don't wreck his fence."

Lauren searched her mind for the name. In five years she'd lost track of people in Masonville. "Tim?"

"Tim Rodgers. He bought the land from my mom after Dad died and she sold the farm. Did you know Garrett tried to buy it from Tim recently?"

"My brother Garrett? He's never farmed in his life. What would he want with a quarter section of pasture?"

Cole shrugged. "I don't know, maybe raise some stock. Now he's out of the military, I guess he's trying to figure out what to do with his life. Unfortunately, Tim's son decided to run cattle here, so Garrett didn't get the land."

Garrett hadn't shared his plans, or his dreams, with her. She'd missed many events in the lives of her brother and sister in the last five years, and she ached with the hurt of it.

Lauren jumped to her feet, too restless to sit. "Do you remember the Halloween Billy TP'd the principal's house? Mr. Schneider nearly had a stroke, he was so mad."

Cole gave a melancholy laugh. "Mostly I remember that Billy talked me into helping him do the deed. He managed to convince everybody at school that some kids from Bismarck had done it. Only the three of us—you and me and Billy—knew the truth."

"And then Billy organized a group of us to take the TP out of Mr. Schneider's trees. Everyone thought he was some kind of hero."

"Yeah, he got a charge out of that. He enjoyed pulling the wool over everyone's eyes," Cole said. "At least the toilet paper didn't stay in Mr. Schneider's trees all winter."

"Yeah." Billy had been a contradiction, even as a teenager. But she'd only seen his charming side. She'd thought he was wonderful, perfect.

Lauren wrapped her arms around herself as she paced, suddenly feeling cold despite the warm evening. Cole picked up his jacket and stood to place it over her shoulders.

"Is that better?"

"Yes. Thank you."

She walked around the ring of stones that had contained countless campfires. In her mind's eye she saw the dead ashes flame to life once more. "I got drunk for the first time here. Do you remember? Billy got hold of a bottle of whiskey from somewhere, and we drank the whole thing. I think I threw up in the trees over there by the couch. As I recall, you held back my hair."

"I remember," he said with a chuckle. "You nearly threw up on my shoes. We had to sober you up before we could take you home."

"I was hung over the next day. I told my mom I had the flu, but she didn't buy it. She made me scrub toilets and wash floors."

"My dad used to make me hoe potatoes in the garden whenever I was hung over." He sighed. "Damn, I miss him."

Lauren pulled Cole's jacket a little closer. Billy could be so sweet, so caring. She could almost hear his laugh, see his face. That was the Billy she'd loved, the boy who'd brought her here, just the two of them, and made love to her for the first time. The boy who'd held her and told her he loved her.

That was the Billy she wanted to remember. Not the man he became.

If they hadn't fought that last time, would he still be alive? She'd told him their marriage was over, that she never wanted to see him again. As far as she was concerned, he was dead to her. She was tormented by the thought that their argument had upset him as much as it had her. Had her ugly words caused him to lose his concentration on the road?

The sudden sob came from deep inside and surprised her with the strength of its emotion. Lauren covered her mouth with her hand, trying to contain the hurt and anguish and raw pain. But now that the tears had started, she couldn't stem the flow. A complicated mixture of grief and anger and guilt poured out of her in wave after wave of agony.

Cole wrapped her in his arms. He held her securely, whispering reassurances.

"It's all right, Lauren. Don't cry. It's going to be okay, sweetheart."

She clung to him, her face buried against his neck. How wonderful to be held, to be touched. It had been so long—

What was she doing? This was Cole, her friend. She pulled away from him. "I'm sorry."

"You don't have anything to apologize for."

She turned away and tried to wipe the tears from her face. After she got her tears under control, she made herself smile at him. "Do you remember the homecoming dance? The time I tripped in my new high heels and sprained my ankle?"

"Of course I do. You couldn't walk, so I carried you from the school gym to Billy's car, and he drove you home. I remember you were a lot heavier than you looked."

She swatted his shoulder, hiccupping laughter mixing with her tears. "Very funny. I was trying to make a point."

He wiped the tears from her cheek with the pad of his thumb, his dark eyes full of tenderness. "So what was your point?"

"You're a good friend. You've always been there every time I've needed you, and here you are again. Thank you."

He stared into her eyes, but said nothing. She couldn't look away. He continued to stroke her cheek with his thumb, the tiny caress acting like a balm to her battered heart. She placed her hand on his cheek.

"Cole."

They reached for each other in mutual need. He pulled her against his chest, his mouth descending on hers in a hungry, urgent kiss. She sighed against his mouth, and he brought her closer. *He wants me.* It had been so long since someone had wanted her. Only her.

They shed their clothes in a flurry of restless touches. In minutes, Lauren's black funeral dress lay on the ground next to Cole's white dress shirt. He kissed her again, his hands sliding up her ribcage to cup her breasts. She slid impatient hands over his broad shoulders, his muscled back, the curve of his buttocks. His skin was as smooth and hard as glass, but hot to the touch. She wanted more of his heat, more of his touch.

More of everything.

She wanted to feel alive again.

His erection pushed against her stomach, and her body shivered with excitement. The evidence of his desire emboldened her.

"You want me," she whispered.

"Yes." His voice was rough with need. "Lauren. Beautiful Lauren."

He held her close and kissed her, and for the first time in a very long time, she felt cherished.

Important.

Loved.

Cole lowered her to the ground, the dried grass and leaves forming a bed beneath them. Then he was inside her, filling all her empty spaces. Joy flooded her heart as her climax built. Each thrust brought her closer to fulfillment, to happiness.

Her orgasm came suddenly, shattering her into tiny pieces. Her body shuddered.

"Cole!"

A moment later he reached his own climax. She held him tightly as tears poured down her face and sobs shook her body. She had no idea why she was crying. What they'd shared had been so beautiful, so amazing. There was no need for tears. But still, they kept coming.

Cole's body tensed. He pulled back and stared into her face. In the fading light, Lauren caught the look of pain in his eyes before he pushed away and began rifling through his clothes.

Her heart sank. *He's sorry he made love to me.*

For a moment she thought she'd be sick. Her stomach roiled, and her heart banged against her ribs. Cole avoided her gaze, presenting his back to her as he yanked on his clothes. Lauren swallowed and reached for her own clothing, getting to her feet on unsteady legs.

Had she disgusted him by reaching for him today, of all days? She was afraid she'd lost her best and oldest friend.

Once he was fully dressed, Cole finally looked at her. "We need to go. You should get back to your family."

Lauren nodded, unable to speak. She followed him out of the trees, back to the fence where their vehicles were parked. Cole held the strands of barbed wire apart so she could slip between them. Once through, she stumbled toward her mother's car and reached for the door handle.

"Lauren, wait."

She dared a glance. His expression was full of anguish, and her heart clenched. The last thing she'd wanted was to cause him pain.

"What happened here," he began, his voice gruff with emotion, "it was…we made a mistake. We were both grieving, maybe a little out of our minds."

Lauren nodded, desperately holding back her tears. She'd made such a mess of things. Cole must hate her for throwing herself at him the way she had. She hated herself, too.

"I'm sorry," he said softly.

The stupid tears burned behind her eyes, but she held them back. She fumbled blindly for the door handle, needing to get away before she broke down in front of him. As she got behind the wheel and started the car, Cole drove away in a cloud of dust.

Lauren rested her head against the steering wheel and cried. She cried for Billy and the loss of the love she'd thought would last a lifetime. But mostly she cried tears of humiliation. Cole must think she was a terrible, terrible person.

And he'd be absolutely right. What kind of woman makes love to her husband's brother on the day of his funeral?

Chapter Two

November 1

"It's confirmed, Lauren. You're pregnant."

Lauren stared at Dr. McKenzie in shock. Even though the evidence had been staring her in the face for weeks—the absence of her period, the tender breasts, the morning nausea—she hadn't quite believed it until this moment. She hadn't dared to believe it.

Elation filled her. She'd wanted a baby, very much, but after two miscarriages she'd given up hope. Now her dream of having a child was coming true.

Reality charged back with a vengeance. Her husband was dead. How the hell was she going to explain being pregnant? The thought had her crashing back to earth.

The idea of telling her family she'd become pregnant on the day of her husband's funeral overwhelmed her with humiliation. Her parents would be so disappointed in her. And her mother-in-law—she couldn't imagine what Ella would say.

Dear God, how would she tell Cole? The only certainty was that this baby was his.

Dr. McKenzie picked up on her confused thoughts. He gave her a kind smile. "Are you planning to continue the pregnancy, Lauren?"

Comprehension came slowly. She stared at him as

his meaning became clear. “Yes, of course I’m continuing the pregnancy! I would never…” She couldn’t say the word *abortion.*

“I’m sorry, but the news didn’t appear to be altogether welcome.”

“It’s very welcome. I guess I’m in a bit of shock right now. It’s complicated.”

He nodded. “I understand your husband passed away recently.”

“Yes, in the summer, at the end of July.”

“I’m sorry for your loss.”

She swallowed. She needed to tell someone the truth, desperately wanted to confide her fears. Charlotte and her mother would be so disappointed if she told them what she’d done. Looking into the doctor’s kind eyes, she decided to trust him. “The child’s not his. That’s why it’s complicated.”

If he was shocked, he didn’t show it. He simply nodded in understanding, as if his female patients told him every day they were having babies they hadn’t conceived with their husbands.

“From the dates you’ve given me I estimate you’re about twelve weeks pregnant.”

“Yes.” It was twelve weeks and three days since Billy’s funeral. Since she’d had sex with Cole.

“Nothing you tell me will leave this room. Anytime you want to talk, I’m here.”

“Thank you, I appreciate the offer. Maybe sometime I’ll take you up on it.”

“Good. Do you have any questions for me?”

“Yes. I had two miscarriages previously, both before twelve weeks of pregnancy, so I’m concerned the same thing will happen again.”

"Even with two miscarriages, especially since they were early miscarriages, your chances of giving birth to a healthy full-term baby aren't much different than if you'd never miscarried at all. You're already at twelve weeks, so my guess is that the danger period has already passed for you."

Lauren released a relieved breath. After her second miscarriage, early in her marriage, she'd tried to get pregnant again but it hadn't happened. As the months and years went by, she'd given up hope of having a family. Though heartbreaking, she came to realize it was for the best. Bringing a baby into her floundering relationship with Billy would have been a mistake.

She'd been given a second chance. Despite everything, her pregnancy was a wonderful, much-wished-for miracle.

"Thank you, Dr. McKenzie. I can assure you this baby is very much wanted."

"I'm glad you're happy about the pregnancy, Lauren. There's no reason to believe you won't give birth to a healthy baby."

She left the doctor's office in something of a daze. Her head spun. Dr. McKenzie wanted her to begin pre-natal vitamins, but she couldn't simply go downtown and pick them up at the drugstore. If someone she knew saw her, news of her pregnancy would spread through Masonville before she got back to her car.

She had to tell everyone. Soon.

Lauren got into her mother's Civic, which she'd borrowed once again, and turned on the ignition. For a moment she sat behind the wheel and stared unseeing at the Masonville Family Health Clinic. As soon as she got back to Charlotte's house, where she'd been living since the funeral, she'd phone her parents and her brother Garrett and ask them to come over. Charlotte was off work at four, so she'd be available this evening. Her sister, a nurse, already suspected something. It was difficult to hide the fact that she started every morning by throwing up, considering they lived together in Charlotte's nine-hundred-square-foot, one-bathroom house. She couldn't hide her morning sickness, or her pregnancy, much longer.

She'd have to call Ella, too. Lauren shivered involuntarily. It was going to be difficult to tell Billy's mother she was pregnant with Cole's child. But she'd be happy, wouldn't she? After all, this baby was still her grandchild.

She sighed. Ella likely wouldn't see things that way. Billy had been her favorite. No matter what he did, he could do no wrong in her eyes. He'd been her golden boy.

That had been the problem.

But before she told anyone else, she had to tell Cole. He deserved to know first.

Once she got back to Charlotte's house, she looked up the number of the veterinary clinic where Cole worked. She dialed the number and a receptionist answered on the second ring.

"Masonville Veterinary Clinic. How can I help you?"

Lauren's mouth was impossibly dry, her voice rusty. "I'd like to speak to Dr. Walsh, please."

"I'm sorry, Dr. Walsh is away this week at a veterinary conference. Can one of the other vets help you?"

"No, that's fine. Thank you very much." She

quickly hung up the phone. Now what did she do?

****

Five days later, Lauren cleared the dishes from Table Fourteen and wiped away the crumbs. As the smell of frying bacon reached her, a sudden wave of nausea struck. She leaned against the table for support, trying to look inconspicuous as she pulled a dry saltine cracker from the pocket of her apron and slowly ate it. Why hadn't she changed shifts with one of the other waitresses? The early morning breakfast shift at the Homestead Restaurant, her place of employment for the past three months, was hectic. She didn't have time to deal with morning sickness. She normally worked the afternoon shift, giving her the luxury of throwing up at home. But her boss, Jenny, had scheduled her for this morning shift since one of the other waitresses had a dental appointment in Bismarck. She should have explained to Jenny, said something.

Something like, "Sorry, Jenny, I can't work the morning shift because I screwed my brother-in-law before my dead husband's body was cold in the ground, and now I'm knocked up and barf my guts out every morning."

Right. That's what she should have said.

"Can we have some more coffee over here?"

Lauren swallowed the last of the dry cracker. "Be right there."

The cracker succeeded in tamping down the nausea. Lauren picked up a full pot of freshly brewed coffee and pasted a smile on her face as she refilled cups in her section.

"Lauren, honey, can you refill coffees at Table Ten in my section?" Greta Peters breezed by carrying five plates of food. Lauren marveled at her sense of balance. She had trouble handling two plates without spillage.

"Sure."

"Love ya, sweetie."

Lauren headed to Greta's section. She'd known Greta since high school. She was an inveterate gossip, and often spoke before she thought, but she had a big heart and a generous spirit. She was the one who'd convinced Jenny to hire Lauren when she needed a job fast. She would always be grateful to her.

As she refilled the coffee cups of the patrons at Table Ten, one of the customers dipped his toast into the yolk of his sunny-side-up egg. The yolk burst open and runny yellow ooze spread across the plate. The smell of eggs and greasy sausage links smacked her in the face.

Bile rose in Lauren's throat, and this time no amount of saltine cracker was going to keep it down. She set the coffeepot on the table with a thud and ran to the bathroom, one hand covering her mouth.

"Lauren? What's wrong, sweetie?" Greta called as she ran by.

Lauren ignored her. She barely made it to the bathroom in time. After emptying the contents of her stomach into the toilet, mostly crackers and bile, she leaned her forehead against the cool porcelain. She couldn't muster the strength to care that she was up close and personal with a public toilet.

The outer door of the bathroom opened, and a knock sounded on her cubicle.

"For goodness' sake! Why didn't you tell us?" Greta called.

Lauren cautiously lifted head. "Tell you what?"

"That you're pregnant, of course!"

Oh, God. If Greta figured it out, how long till others did?

More to the point, if Greta realized she was pregnant, how long till she told all of Masonville?

"You can't tell anyone," she whispered, pushing herself to her feet and opening the cubicle door. The nausea had passed. It usually did once she vomited. "I haven't had a chance to tell my family yet."

"I knew you were pregnant!" Greta said triumphantly. Her gaze slid to Lauren's abdomen. "I thought I detected a baby bump."

Lauren looked at her reflection in the bathroom mirror. "A baby bump?" Elation filled her. Her baby was growing. *All the more reason to tell her family. And Cole.*

"Well, it was either a baby bump or you were getting fat." Greta clasped both of Lauren's hands in hers, her expression wistful. "I'm so happy for you, sweetie. I know how much you loved Billy. At least you'll have his baby."

She stared at Greta. *Billy's baby?* A part of her wanted to set Greta straight, but the coward in her spoke first. "Yes. I will."

She hated herself in that moment. But she couldn't tell Greta who the father of her baby really was.

Greta squeezed her hands before letting go. "Are you feeling up to going back out there?"

"Yes, I'm fine now." She grasped Greta's arm before she could open the bathroom door. "You can't tell anyone. Promise me, Greta."

Greta frowned, her brow wrinkling as if she were waging an internal battle between her angels and her demons.

"I promise," she said at last. She didn't look happy about it. This was probably the juiciest gossip she'd heard in months.

Lauren washed her hands and ran a wet paper towel across her face before reentering the diner with Greta. The whole place went quiet, and all eyes turned toward them. Greta put her hands on her hips, one eyebrow raised.

"We washed our hands, if that's what you're worried about."

There were a few chuckles and guilty looks before everyone went back to their breakfasts. Lauren gratefully returned to pouring coffee and taking orders. A moment later the little bell over the door rang and she looked up to see Cole enter the diner with one of the other vets from the clinic. Her heart made a little stutter-step. She stared at him a moment, and he acknowledged her with a curt nod before sitting down with his breakfast companion. In the three months since they'd made love, nods like this were the only communication between them. They hadn't spoken since the day they'd made a baby together.

Guilt clogged Lauren's throat, and she had to make herself look away and get back to work.

He deserves to know the truth.

She wanted to tell him. For five days, Lauren had waited on pins and needles for Cole to return to Masonville from his conference. She hadn't been able to sleep worrying about his reaction to her news. Cole was a good person, but she couldn't predict whether he'd be happy about the baby. This pregnancy would change his life in ways he might not expect or want.

Whatever his reaction, he had to be told. As soon as she finished her shift, she'd call him and arrange to meet. This wasn't the kind of news she could deliver over the phone.

Isabelle rang the bell in the kitchen that signaled an order was ready.

"Order's up, Lauren," she called.

Lauren went to collect it, grabbing a large tray on her way. She arranged the plates on the tray and lifted it, staggering a little under the weight. Perhaps she should have made two trips. She gritted her teeth and kept walking.

"Lauren! What are you doing?" Greta bustled over, wagging a finger at her. "You shouldn't be lifting something this heavy."

"Shhh! Keep your voice down."

Greta shot her an annoyed look, but she lowered her voice. "Fine. But if something happens, don't tell me I didn't warn you."

That gave Lauren pause. She couldn't bear to go through a third miscarriage. The disappointment, the grief, the *emptiness* had nearly killed her. She wanted this baby more than she'd ever wanted anything in this world.

"Could you take some of the plates? It is kind of heavy."

Greta smiled brightly. "Of course, sweetie." She began removing plates from the tray. "Where to?"

"Table Eight."

Lauren set her tray on the edge of Table Eight, passed the plates to their proper owners, and did the same with the plates that Greta carried.

"Enjoy your breakfast. I'll be around with more

coffee in a few moments."

As she turned to leave, an older woman at a nearby table touched her arm.

"Lauren dear, I'm so happy to see you. Do you remember me? I'm Elizabeth, Ella Walsh's sister. I wasn't able to attend Billy's funeral and didn't get a chance to extend my condolences to you. I'm so sorry."

Lauren dipped her head in what she hoped was a respectful nod. "Yes, of course I remember you. Thank you."

"He was quite a young man, so vital, so ambitious."

"Yes." Lauren was aware that Greta hovered nearby, listening to every word. How soon could she politely slip away?

"Ella is devastated, of course. I don't think she'll ever get over his death."

"No, I don't think she will."

Greta stepped forward, placing a hand on Elizabeth's shoulder. "Don't worry. Ella will be fine. She's soon going to get some very good news."

Lauren's face grew hot, and she grasped the back of a chair as a wave of dizziness swept over her. She should have known Greta couldn't keep her mouth shut for more than five minutes.

"What does she mean, Lauren?" Elizabeth asked, confusion on her face. Her eyes suddenly widened and her gaze drifted to Lauren's belly. "Are you saying there's a baby? Billy's baby?"

Jenny walked by with a pot of coffee. "Who's having a baby?"

"Lauren is, aren't you, dear?" Elizabeth stood and placed her hand on her arm. "You're having my nephew's child."

"Yes, I am."

Lauren rationalized that she was telling the truth. She *was* pregnant, and the baby *was* Elizabeth's nephew's child. Only, she hadn't specified which nephew.

A lie is a lie, her heart told her. But standing here in her hometown, with dozens of her fellow Masonvillers watching, she found she lacked the courage to tell the truth. It was too humiliating. Her reputation would be ruined in this town forever.

"Did you hear that, everyone?" Jenny said, addressing the diner's inhabitants. "Our Lauren is having Billy Walsh's baby!"

A cheer rose from the locals. Billy had been a hero to many. A local boy who'd done good.

She lifted her head and her gaze collided with Cole's. He looked shocked, stunned, bewildered. And she read the question in his eyes.

Is the baby mine?

Lauren swallowed and looked away, her heart crying. How could she ever tell Cole the truth now?

Chapter Three

November 5

Cole left the diner in a daze. Lauren was pregnant. With Billy's baby.

Was it really Billy's?

He chided himself for his elation at the thought that Lauren could be carrying his child. It *wasn't* his baby. Billy and Lauren had been married for over five years. Of course it was Billy's baby.

They'd only made love once, but he hadn't used birth control. Lauren had caught him off guard. Perhaps she'd caught herself off guard, too. He remembered her tears after they'd made love. She'd wished it hadn't happened. It had nearly killed him to see those tears of regret.

Of shame.

He could have said no. He could have simply taken her home to her mother. Instead he'd taken advantage of her at her most vulnerable.

He'd been a selfish prick.

Cole had chastised himself over and over. But the truth was, he hadn't wanted to say no to Lauren. He'd wanted her on the day of Billy's funeral the same way he'd wanted her since he was sixteen years old.

He loved her. He'd always loved her. More fool him.

Lauren had been fourteen and already a beauty when Cole fell in love with her. He was sixteen and a half, serious and shy, his attention focused on his goal of becoming a veterinarian. He spent hours studying so he'd get the good marks he needed to get into veterinary college, especially his first choice, Purdue University. He'd needed money to go away to school, too, so to supplement his part-time after-school job bagging groceries at a local supermarket, he tutored other students in math, biology, and chemistry, his best subjects.

One day Lauren stepped into the high school office he used for his noon-hour tutoring sessions. And his life was never the same.

They'd become friends. She was sweet and funny and kind, not the least bit stuck-up like some pretty girls. He'd even worked up the courage to ask her out on a couple of movie dates. But he'd been too shy to even hold her hand, much less kiss her.

One Saturday Lauren came to his house on the farm for a chemistry tutoring session. Billy had answered the door. They'd known each other, of course. They were the same age, and Masonville was a small town of less than six thousand. But it wasn't until Billy realized Cole had a thing for her that he began to pursue her.

Cole sighed as he dug his keys from his pocket and headed to his truck. That was the kind of relationship he'd had with his brother. They were always competing with each other, in sports, in school, for their parents' attention. And eventually for Lauren. It was a fight he knew he'd lose.

Billy had been handsome, charming, funny.

Everyone loved him. He only had to produce his lopsided grin and all sins were forgiven, no matter what offense he might have committed. Small wonder Lauren had fallen for him.

At first, the three of them hung around together, swimming in the summer, skating outdoors on a frozen pond in the winter. Then there was their secret hideout in the pasture, the place where all three of them tried their first cigarette, their first beer. But eventually, Billy and Lauren didn't ask him to join them anymore.

He'd hoped that someday Lauren would to able to look at him without being blinded by Billy's shining light. He wanted her to see him, to love him. But those hopes died when Lauren married Billy three years after they finished high school.

The news of their marriage had caught Cole by surprise. They'd gone separate ways after high school, Lauren to college in Minot and Billy to the University of North Dakota in Grand Forks to play hockey. He'd heard from his mother that Billy was dating a new girl, Mia Cottrell from Masonville, who was also going to college there. Cole had been away at school in Indiana at the time, but he'd rejoiced at the news.

The next thing he heard, Billy and Lauren were married. The day he'd received the news, he got blindingly, spectacularly drunk and stayed that way for two days, until the pain had subsided into a dull ache he could deal with. After that, he made himself date other girls, but none of them made him forget his feelings for Lauren.

All his memories of his brother were interwoven with jealousy and anger, even hate. How could you love someone and hate them at the same time?

Despite all Billy's charm, Cole understood better than anyone how selfish he could be. Lauren had been married to him for five years. He'd never once heard her complain about Billy's behavior. She must have truly loved him to stay with him that long. But if that was the truth, why had she made love with him?

He'd relived those moments with Lauren over and over—the softness of her skin, her sweet scent, the desire in her touch. For a few shining moments he'd believed she wanted him, too. Until he saw her tears. She'd been grieving, and he'd taken advantage. Worse, she'd regretted what they'd done, almost immediately.

Cole opened the door to his truck and got behind the wheel. She'd made love to him because she was hurting and he happened to be there. Nothing more.

He didn't have any better chance with her now than he'd had back in high school. Billy's ghost would always come between them.

****

Lauren hadn't been home five minutes before her mother phoned. Grace Saunders didn't waste time on preliminaries.

"Why did I have to hear from my hairdresser that my daughter is pregnant?"

She winced. "That wasn't my intention, Mom. Greta kind of spilled the beans at work today."

She explained what happened. "I was going to tell everyone at the same time—you and Dad and Charlotte and Garrett. I was waiting."

"Waiting for what?"

She couldn't tell her she'd been waiting to talk to Cole first. So she told a half-truth. "I was waiting to see if I was going to lose this pregnancy, too."

"Oh, honey. I'm sorry. Everything's going to work out fine this time. You'll see."

Lauren struggled to keep the tears at bay. Everything made her cry these days. "Yes, I think it will turn out, too. It feels different this time."

"Good. Have you told your brother and sister yet?"

"No, but I think Charlotte suspects. I'll tell her as soon as she gets home. Garrett doesn't know, unless he heard what happened at the diner today."

"Call him. He deserves to hear the straight goods from you."

Lauren nearly burst into tears at her mother's words. *He deserves to hear the straight goods from you.* Cole deserved that, too. But how could she tell him the truth when the whole town believed a lie?

It was her fault that everyone believed a lie. She'd been too scared, too embarrassed, to tell the truth.

"What about Ella? Have you talked to her?"

She shuddered. Talking to Ella about this baby was the last thing she wanted to do. "No, but I imagine her sister has filled her in."

"Would you like me to talk to her?"

For one frantic moment, she nearly said yes. It would be so much easier to have her mom deal with Ella. But that was the coward's way out, and she'd already been cowardly enough.

"Thanks, Mom, but this is something I need to do myself."

"Of course, sweetheart. I know she can be…difficult, but she needs to hear the news from you. She'll likely want to know when the baby is due. So do I, actually."

"The baby's due…March twenty-second."

She hoped her mother didn't hear the hesitation in her voice. Or the lie. Dr. McKenzie had told her that based on her last period, her due date would be around April twenty-second. But it didn't take a genius to do the math and figure out that using that due date, Billy would have already been dead by the time she conceived. So she lied.

Lie upon lie.

"I'm so happy for you, Lauren. I know how much you've wanted a baby, and I know you and Billy had your ups and downs, but this baby is like a precious gift. Billy's last gift to you."

"Yes." She nearly choked on the word. Her mother was aware they'd had problems, but she didn't know the full extent. She had no idea about Billy's affairs. Lauren had been too ashamed, too embarrassed, to confide in her, or anyone else.

"We're here for you, honey. I don't want you to worry about anything."

Too late. As if worrying about the whole town of Masonville discovering the real identity of her baby's father wasn't enough, she had to worry about how she'd provide for her child. She enjoyed working in the diner, but she didn't make enough money to pay for all the needs of a baby. She didn't want her child growing up in poverty, or both of them living with her parents or her sister and dependent on them. She had to figure out what to do next.

Her child needed her to make good choices.

****

Lauren pulled up in front of her mother-in-law's apartment and turned off the ignition. Stalling, she sat behind the wheel and stared at the building. She dreaded speaking to Ella, but that was nothing new. Her mother-in-law had never believed she was good enough for Billy. After all, she was the one who'd trapped him into marriage by getting pregnant.

With a sigh, she opened the car door and got out, knowing she couldn't put off this meeting any longer.

In the small foyer of the apartment building, she hit the button for Ella's apartment. She heard her mother-in-law's voice through the speaker. "Yes?"

"Ella, it's Lauren."

"I'll buzz you right in."

The buzzer sounded, and she pulled open the door. She walked up the two flights of stairs to Ella's apartment rather than take the elevator. *More stalling, Lauren?*

As she reached the apartment, she saw Ella at the door, waiting. "What took you so long? Has the elevator stopped working?"

"No, I walked up the stairs."

"The stairs?" Ella frowned. "For goodness' sake, girl. You can't go trotting up and down the stairs. Are you trying to have another miscarriage?"

"No, of course not." It hurt that she would even suggest such a thing, especially in the hallway where all her neighbors could hear. Ella knew about her first miscarriage, since her pregnancy had triggered the marriage, but Lauren had only confided in her mother and sister after the second miscarriage. "Do you think we could speak inside?"

With a pinched expression, Ella stepped aside and allowed her in. Her apartment was small and cramped, filled with memorabilia from Billy's hockey career. One wall was covered with photos of him at various ages in the uniforms of the different teams he'd played with. Billy's trophies and awards filled her bookshelves to overflowing. Lauren didn't see one piece of memorabilia from Cole's youth. It was as if Ella had only one son.

Lauren removed her jacket and tossed it over a chair. "You don't need to worry. I'm taking excellent care of myself. My baby's health means everything to me."

"Well, I'm glad to hear it. That baby is all I have left of Billy." Ella's face was raw with grief, as if Billy's death had happened only yesterday. She roused herself after a moment. "Would you like tea?"

Lauren nodded politely. "That would be lovely. Thank you."

While Ella shuffled around the kitchen, Lauren explored the small apartment. It had a small galley kitchen which opened up on one end to an eating area. The living room was adjacent to the dining area and had sliding glass doors out to a balcony. Though small, the apartment was bright and sunny and reasonably new. She'd only been here briefly once before, about three years previously, a few months after Billy's father died. Ella had sold the farm where the boys grew up, and Cole had moved her out of the farmhouse and found this apartment for her. At least in the apartment she didn't have to worry about mowing grass or shoveling snow. Cole was a good son, even if Ella didn't acknowledge the fact.

Ella brought cups and saucers to the table along with a teapot. She poured tea in both cups before sitting. Lauren sat in the chair across from her, her hands clutched in her lap.

"When are you due?"

Lauren swallowed and forced herself to meet Ella's gaze. "In March. The twenty-second." She cringed at the lie.

Ella nodded and lifted her cup to her lips. After taking a sip, she set it carefully in the saucer again. "And the pregnancy is going well?"

"Yes. My doctor tells me everything is normal."

"That's good."

Lauren lifted her teacup and drank. The meeting was going pretty much the way she'd expected. Aside from the baby, they had very little to say to each other.

"Billy was my life," Ella said. Her teacup wobbled in her hand. "With this baby, it's almost as if a part of him will live on." She sniffed, holding back tears. "I miss him so much."

"I know you do, Ella. I'm sorry."

Her mother-in-law would probably grieve for Billy for the rest of her life. Lauren's grieving period was already over. Guilt washed over her at that acknowledgement. She had the baby to think of and a living to make, but the truth was that she had grieved—for the end of her marriage and for the person Billy had been—long before he died. The only emotion left was relief that her marriage was over. And that made her feel even more guilty.

"I hope you won't keep me from seeing my grandchild. I have a right to know Billy's child."

Anger glittered in her former mother-in-law's eyes, as if she expected to be rebuffed. Lauren wondered what Billy had told her about their marriage, about her, over the years. Of course, Ella had never needed a reason to think the worst of her.

She nodded coolly. "I never considered denying you access to the baby, Ella. I want my child to know all her grandparents."

Even though the baby she carried wasn't Billy's child, she was still Ella's grandchild. She suppressed a shiver at the thought of her reaction if she ever discovered the truth. She didn't care if Ella hated her, but she wouldn't tolerate her taking out her anger on her child. Lauren placed a hand on her belly and made a silent vow.

I won't let anyone hurt you.

****

Lauren finished wiping the table, then paused, both hands braced on the table top and her head bowed. A delightful accompaniment to her morning sickness was a bone-weary tiredness that made her want to curl into a ball and nap every afternoon. She swore that if she ever had the chance she'd sleep for a week.

Fat chance of it, though. Most nights she couldn't sleep more than two or three hours before having to get up to pee. Aside from the morning sickness, the fatigue, the heartburn, and the overactive bladder, she was doing great.

And she wouldn't have it any other way. This baby meant too much to her.

"You okay?"

Lauren looked up to see Jenny staring at her in concern.

"I'm fine. Just tired."

"Believe it or not, I can remember way back to the time I was having my babies. I know how it is. I had six pregnancies, each one worse than the one before."

"You're not making me feel better, Jenny."

She grinned. "Sorry. It does get better in the second trimester."

"That's a relief."

Greta joined them, a coffeepot in one hand. "What's the meeting about, ladies?"

"We're comparing war stories about pregnancies," Jenny said.

Greta put down her pot and placed her hand on her hip. "I tell you, with my second, I had the mother of all labors, pardon the pun. Twenty-two hours of pushing. After Jacob was born, I told the doctor to sew up that business down there because I was never going to use it again."

Jenny barked with laughter. Despite her fatigue, Lauren couldn't help smiling at that bit of news.

"I hope you changed your mind about using your equipment again," Jenny said, wiping a tear from the corner of her eye.

"Once I switched from procreation to recreation, everything was fine."

This time Lauren laughed out loud.

Greta examined her closely. "You look like hell, sweetie."

"Gee, thanks."

"Why don't you sit down for a minute, put your feet up?" Jenny coaxed. "The supper crowd won't be around for a few minutes yet."

Lauren gratefully slid into a booth and put her feet up. Greta probed her ankles with gentle fingers. "Your ankles are a little puffy. That probably means you should stay off your feet."

"Unless you plan to wheel me around on a gurney from table to table, I don't think that's an option."

"Greta's right, Lauren. You need to look after yourself."

Her stomach swooped, anxiety making her feel nauseated again. "You're not going to fire me, are you, Jenny?"

"Of course not. But maybe you want to think about cutting back your hours, or even looking for a job where you don't need to be on your feet so much."

"I can't afford to cut back my hours. I need to provide for the baby. I can't live with my sister forever. I should get my own place. Someplace nice for the baby." She couldn't help the note of panic that seeped into her voice.

"I know," Jenny said soothingly. "We'll figure something out."

People began filing into the diner. Lauren sighed and pushed herself out of the booth. *No more lounging for you, kid. If you want to keep your job, it's back to work.*

Still, she knew Jenny was right. She couldn't do anything to jeopardize the health of her baby.

A short time later, Cole, along with several people from the veterinary clinic, trouped into the diner and seated themselves in one of the larger booths at the back. Cole's eyes met hers, and he gave her his customary nod. Lauren nodded back, her heart heavy. For years, they'd had such an easy friendship. They'd been so close at one time, the three of them. Even after she and Billy were together, her friendship with Cole had remained strong. She'd phoned him often, especially when she was lonely and needed someone to talk to. Not to complain about Billy and their nomadic life, but to hear a friendly voice and share a laugh. She wished she could go back to that friendship. Through the rocky parts of her marriage, Cole had been her anchor, someone she could always depend on.

Until she'd ruined their friendship.

She missed him. She missed talking to him, hearing his voice, seeing his quick smile. Cole had the most beautiful smile, the most beautiful mouth. The natural curve of his lips was so masculine, so sensual...

She remembered his kiss, his mouth hot on hers. He'd caressed the nape of her neck, bringing her closer. He tasted of mint, so sweet and fresh and delicious—

"Lauren, can you make sure the people at Table Five have water and menus?" Jenny said, breaking into her memories.

"Yes, of course."

She grabbed some menus and went into work mode, shoving the memory of Cole's kiss to the recesses of her mind. Despite everything, she couldn't be sorry she'd made love with him. For a few brief moments, he'd made her feel cherished. It had been a long time since she'd been special to someone. And he'd given her a child, the most precious gift she could ever receive. Someday she'd tell him the truth, once she was stronger. He deserved to know.

Business was brisk tonight. Lauren tried to keep up, but she was so tired. And her feet hurt. During a lull, she slipped into the back room and sat down, taking off her shoes and rubbing her feet.

"This isn't going to work, sweetie."

Greta gave her arm an affectionate squeeze. Lauren almost cried, knowing she was right.

"What isn't going to work?" Jenny asked.

"Little Mama here shouldn't be on her feet so

much. She should be taking better care of herself."

"I have to work," Lauren said. "I don't have a choice."

"Maybe you do," Jenny said. "The receptionist at the veterinary clinic is leaving. She's going to California with her boyfriend. That's why the whole office is here today. It's her last day."

"You could do that job," Greta said.

"No." Considering the current state of their relationship, working with Cole every day would be difficult for both of them. She couldn't subject him to her unwanted presence at his place of business.

"Of course you could," Greta said, misunderstanding Lauren's refusal. "You're a bright girl. Besides, your brother-in-law works there. He'll put in a good word for you. You're a shoo-in."

"I don't want to impose on Cole. I'd only want a job I got on my own merit, not because someone felt sorry for me."

Greta patted her shoulder. "I understand, sweetie. You're shy about asking for help. So maybe your friends have to ask for you."

With that she marched back into the diner. Lauren got to her feet, alarmed. What the hell was she planning to do?

As Lauren reentered the diner, she saw Greta pouring coffee at Cole's table. She stood behind the drink machine at the counter, where she could watch without being seen.

"Congratulations, Suzy. I'm sure you'll love sunny California," Greta was saying. She paused, the coffeepot in one hand. "So have you hired anyone to take Suzy's place?"

"No, not yet," said Dr. Waverly, the owner of the veterinary clinic. He gave the former receptionist a wink. "Suzy didn't give us a lot of notice. We haven't had time to advertise yet."

"I know someone who'd be a wonderful addition to your clinic. She's smart, she knows accounting, and she's great with people."

"Oh, yeah?" Dr. Waverly said. "Who's that?"

"Lauren Walsh."

Lauren almost threw up on her shoes. The heat of embarrassment rose up her chest to her face, and up to her scalp, until she thought the top of her head would blow off. Mortification spread to all her limbs; she was so limp she could barely stand.

Dr. Waverly turned to Cole. "Lauren's your sister-in-law, isn't she?"

"Yes, she is."

"Widowed now, and pregnant?"

"Yes."

He nodded at Greta. "Have her bring in her resume, and we'll take a look at it. I'd like to help her out if I can."

Greta beamed. "Thank you! You won't regret it."

Lauren gripped the edge of the counter. *My God. What has she done?*

Greta stepped behind the counter with a little skip in her gait. She gave Lauren a sassy grin, obviously proud of herself.

"You're welcome!"

Lauren smiled weakly. She had no choice now but to apply for the job at the veterinary clinic. If she didn't, Greta and the others would want to know the reason why, and there was no way she could tell them.

Chapter Four

November 8

Cole dared a glance across the desk at Lauren. She looked ill at ease, and he wondered if working here at the clinic would be the best thing for her after all. He'd convinced Tom Waverly that if she did apply for the job they'd give it to her. He'd extolled her virtues as an honest, hardworking person. He had no doubt she'd be great at the job. Having her work at the clinic would give him the opportunity to keep an eye on her, make sure she looked after herself and was eating properly.

But if his presence caused her discomfort or stress, he'd have to let her go her own way. At the thought of never again seeing Lauren's beautiful smile, of hearing her laugh, of talking to her, his heart constricted painfully. He'd missed her these last three months. He missed her frequent phone calls. He wanted to be there for her, to be her friend, if nothing else.

He'd tried for years to push her out of his heart. It wasn't healthy for him to be in love with another man's wife, especially his brother's. But no matter how many other girls he dated, or slept with, Lauren was always there, firmly entrenched in his soul. He'd come to believe she always would be.

Dr. Waverly read Lauren's neatly typed resume. "I see you have two years of college and a partly finished degree in accounting."

"Yes." Lauren cleared her throat. "I completed two years of my business degree with a major in accounting at Minot State University."

"Why didn't you finish your degree?"

She lifted her chin slightly as if trying to maintain her dignity. "I married my husband at that point, and left school to follow his career. My hope is to someday go back to school to finalize my degree."

Cole hadn't known that finishing school was a goal of hers. She hadn't talked to him about it. For some reason it bothered him that she hadn't shared her dreams with him.

Had she shared them with Billy? Of course, she had. He was only her brother-in-law, her friend. Nothing more.

"Tell me a little about your work experience," Dr. Waverly said.

She recounted the places where she'd worked the last five years. They included restaurants, clothing stores, a hardware store. In most cases she worked the retail end of the business as well as helping out with the bookkeeping, but she'd also worked temporarily as a receptionist in a doctor's office.

"I've learned to be adaptable, organized, and efficient in every job. I had to learn the business quickly, since we were moving around so much." She sounded apologetic for that.

Cole shifted in his chair. It wasn't her fault Billy had constantly uprooted her in a vain attempt to pursue *his* dreams.

"I'm sure you'll be an excellent addition to our clinic, Lauren. I'm especially interested in your bookkeeping abilities. We currently pay a firm to come in and do our day-to-day accounting."

She nodded, looking interested, and asked about the accounting software the clinic used, information Cole had no knowledge of. But she seemed excited, so that made him happy.

Dr. Waverly got to his feet. "I've already spoken to Jenny at the Homestead Restaurant, and she speaks very highly of you. Cole promised me he'd phone the rest of your references. If they check out, we can talk about a start date."

Lauren rose as well, and held out her hand. "Thank you very much for seeing me. I appreciate your kindness."

He shook hands with her, saying, "It's my pleasure. I look forward to having you with us."

With that he left the room, leaving Cole alone with Lauren. She looked around nervously before finally settling her gaze on him. She gave him a tight smile.

"I guess that's my cue to leave."

Cole jumped to his feet. "Why don't you stay while I call your references? We can talk a little more about the job."

In reality, he didn't have a clue what the receptionist did at the clinic, aside from answering the phone. All he knew was that unlike the job at the diner, she didn't have to be on her feet all day.

"Okay." She sat once more, though Cole noticed she was sitting on the edge of her seat as if getting ready to make a speedy getaway. He looked at the three references on her resume, each coming from a different state. She and Billy really *had* moved around. He couldn't imagine how tough that must have been for

Lauren. She'd been far from home and a long way from the support of family and friends, with only Billy to rely on. His brother hadn't been the most supportive, or reliable, person.

"Which one of these references do you want me to phone?" he asked.

She gave him a chiding look. "Cole, you're not supposed to ask a prospective employee that. You're supposed to call all the references to get a balanced opinion."

"I already know they're going to give you glowing reviews."

"How do you know that?"

"Because I know you."

She stared at him a moment, her eyes growing misty. For a moment he thought she was going to cry, but instead she smiled. "Thank you. I appreciate your faith in me. But you really need to call all my references."

"As far as I'm concerned, the job is yours."

"You promised your boss you'd check my references."

He waved his hand. "It's not important."

"It is to me. I don't want this job because you feel sorry for me. If I get this job, I want it to be because I've earned it on my own merits."

Her uncompromising look told him she wasn't kidding. She'd walk if he didn't take this interview seriously.

So he did. He called the hardware store in Georgia and spoke to the owner. She said she wished she could have kept Lauren at her store, but her husband got traded to another team, and they had to move. He got similar stories from the other two references, a women's clothing store in Alabama and the doctor in Louisiana. Lauren's former supervisors spoke of her strong work ethic, her easy way with customers, patients, and co-workers, and her willingness to do whatever was needed to get the job done. They all said they'd hire her back in a heartbeat.

That was good enough for Cole.

"They all loved you and thought you were the best thing since sliced bread. So you're hired. Are you happy now?"

A genuine smile slowly curled her lips. "If this is how you conduct business, you really do need me."

Truer words were never spoken.

"You'll take the job?"

She hesitated. "Only if it's not awkward for you. It might be uncomfortable for you to see me here every day."

"Why would seeing you be uncomfortable for me?" Nothing could be further from the truth.

"Because of what happened." Her gaze skittered away, her voice barely a whisper.

Ah. That. "Lauren. Look at me. Please."

She lifted her gaze to his and he saw her genuine worry. She was concerned for *him*. "I am not going to be uncomfortable having you work here. In fact, I welcome it. I want you to feel comfortable here, too, and to know that you're wanted and needed in our clinic."

Her brow furrowed. "You're sure?"

"Absolutely. Now, will you take the job?"

He held his breath while he waited for her answer. Finally, her lips curved in a tremulous smile.

"Yes, I'll take the job." She held up her hand as he started to speak. "I know you've probably convinced your boss to give me this job because you feel sorry for me, but I'm going to prove to you I can pull my own weight. I'm going to prove I'm the best person for this job."

"I have no doubt you are the best person."

Lauren cocked her head to one side and gazed at him. He wondered what she was thinking. She didn't appear angry with him for taking advantage of her vulnerability on the day of Billy's funeral, though she had every right to be. Did she ever think about what they'd shared the way he did? Did she ever think about making love with him? She'd been so warm and soft and wet, her kisses so sweet. So precious to him. She'd welcomed him into her body—

"Thank you."

Her softly spoken words propelled him back to the present. "For what?"

She blinked a couple of times before answering. "For caring. For being my friend. You are still my friend, aren't you, Cole?"

He couldn't believe she had to ask. "Yes, of course. I'll always be your friend."

"I'm glad. I was afraid…" She shook her head, then looked up with a smile. "I'm glad."

"So am I."

He was profoundly relieved she wasn't angry with him. They were still friends. That was something, he supposed. Not nearly enough, but something.

"When would you like me to start work?"

"Is tomorrow too soon?"

****

Lauren arrived back at Charlotte's house at the same time her sister got home from work. She pulled the Civic behind Charlotte's car and got out, popping the hatch to retrieve the groceries she'd purchased after her interview. Still wearing her scrubs, Charlotte walked over to her car and grabbed one of the bags.

"Hi! How did the interview go?"

"It went great. I got the job."

Charlotte's eyes widened in delight. "That's fantastic! I didn't think they'd make their decision so quickly. Congratulations!"

Lauren closed the hatch, holding her grocery bag and her purse in one hand. "Thanks. I'm sure Cole convinced the owner to hire me."

"He knows you'll be great. Cole is a good friend."

"Yes, he is."

She was so relieved he wasn't angry with her. She prayed they could get their relationship back on its normal, friendly footing.

"I've bought some sparkling cider, non-alcoholic of course, and a couple of small steaks. What do you say we have ourselves a little celebration?"

"I say, let's get this party started!"

While they cooked, they danced around the kitchen, singing along at full volume to songs by Pink and Lady Gaga and Beyoncé. Charlotte's beagle Daisy pranced around them, barking her enthusiasm. Lauren hadn't laughed so much since—she couldn't remember how long it had been since she'd been genuinely happy and having fun. Maybe her life was turning a corner. Maybe she and the baby had a chance for happiness.

They finished cooking and carried their plates to the dining room table. Charlotte cut into her steak and popped a small piece into her mouth.

"Oh, my God, that's so good!" she said, closing her eyes in a blissful expression. "I haven't had steak in ages."

"You haven't gone vegan or something, have you?"

"No, not intentionally. But I hate cooking for myself. I usually end up making a sandwich or a frozen dinner." She stabbed another piece of steak. "That's why I like having you stay with me. You cook."

Lauren smiled fondly at her older sister. "It's my pleasure. I don't know what I would have done these last few months without you."

"I'm glad I was able to help. Truly."

Charlotte had been her rock. She'd given her a home, and held her as she cried. She didn't know how she was ever going to repay her.

"I've been thinking," Lauren began, "now that I'm going to be working at the clinic and making a little more money, I should start paying you rent."

Charlotte put down her fork. "No, absolutely not. I won't take your money."

"But Char—"

"No! You're going to have a baby to look after, and babies need all kinds of stuff, like cribs and diapers, and, I don't know…more diapers. You need to save your money."

"Yeah, but—"

"And didn't you tell me you'd like to go back to school and finish your degree? You need money for that."

She held up her hand. "Charlotte, I love you to pieces, but this is something I have to do. I need to pay my fair share. I won't be able to respect myself if I don't."

"Lauren, come on. I want to help."

She reached across the table to grasp her sister's hand. "You *are* helping. Every day. And I love you for it. But I need to pay you rent."

Charlotte frowned at her, and for a second Lauren thought she'd argue with her again. But instead she sighed and leaned back in her chair. "All right, fine, you can pay rent. But we're going to keep it very low, okay?"

Lauren crossed her arms. "The rent has to be a reasonable amount or it's meaningless."

They spent the next few minutes hashing out terms, until they came to an agreement they could both live with. Charlotte grinned at her.

"You drive a hard bargain. Have you ever considered being a labor negotiator?"

Lauren laughed. "No, the only thing I've ever considered being was an accountant." She tenderly massaged her tiny baby bump. "And a mother."

"It's going to be difficult, but I think you really should consider finishing your degree."

She was right. Her child needed stability, and the only way she was going to be financially stable was if she finished her degree, obtained an accounting designation, and found a well-paying, secure job. She couldn't continue working in entry level, minimum wage jobs. The job at the vet clinic was a step up and she was grateful, but she was capable of so much more.

Her child deserved a good home.

My child deserves to know her father.

The guilty thought caused her appetite to desert

her. Would she ever be brave enough to tell Cole the truth?

The ringing of her phone saved her from answering that question. She picked it up on the second ring.

"Hello?"

"Hello, Lauren? Ella Walsh here. How are you and my grandbaby doing?"

Ella had never been interested in the state of her health before her pregnancy. A ball of anxiety formed in her stomach. "I'm very well, thank you. We both are."

"I'm glad to hear it. I saw a wonderful crib in Bismarck the other day, and I'd be so happy to buy it for my grandchild."

"That's very generous of you, but it's not necessary."

Lauren worried Ella couldn't afford to buy a crib. After she'd sold the farm and settled all the debts, there had been virtually nothing left. Lauren remembered Billy had been angry about that. He'd expected some kind of inheritance, but apparently his father had had to take out a second mortgage after two crop failures in a row. The stress had contributed to his heart attack.

"I had my heart set on buying the crib," Ella said, her voice turning cold. "Couldn't you allow me to do that much, at least, for Billy's baby?"

Lauren closed her eyes and huffed out a breath. She didn't want to have this conversation. If Ella was determined to spend her money, there was nothing she could do about it.

"All right, Ella, if that's what you'd like, I'd be pleased to accept it. Thank you."

"Oh, wonderful! They said at the store they'd have

to order it in. You said the baby was due in March?"

"March, yes." *There was that lie again.*

"Just so you know, I'm ordering it in a dark brown, in case you want to buy other bedroom furniture to go with it."

Lauren dutifully wrote down the brand and model number of the crib so she could look it up online. After she hung up, it occurred to her that Ella hadn't bothered to ask her what kind of crib she would like, or if she wanted it in dark brown. She decided it was easier to accept whatever Ella purchased than to get into an argument with her. It wasn't worth the aggravation. Ella always managed to get whatever she wanted anyway.

She returned to the dining room table and finished the remains of her now cold steak. Charlotte gave her a sympathetic smile.

"What did Ella want?"

Lauren explained about the crib. "She probably can't afford it, but as usual she's determined to have her way."

Charlotte lifted her champagne flute of sparkling cider. "She's an old dog, Lauren. You're not going to teach her new tricks."

"I know you're right, but—"

"No buts, Lauren. Forget about Ella. She has to live with the consequences of her actions. And you, my dear, have a rosy future ahead of you."

"Rosy, huh? Single mother, borrowed car, unable to provide a roof over her child's head without help from her sister. How is that rosy?"

"For the first time in five years, you're free to make your own decisions. I'm confident any decisions you make for yourself and your baby are going to be a hell of lot better than the ones Billy made for you." Charlotte grasped her hand. "I'm sorry to speak ill of the dead, but you know I never liked Billy. I didn't want him to die, though. I'm sorry he's not going to get a chance to see his child."

Charlotte's words pierced Lauren straight through the heart. Tears filled her eyes. She couldn't bring herself to tell Charlotte the truth. She was ashamed of staying in a sham of a marriage for so long, ashamed of being the pathetic, cheated-on wife. She couldn't bear to be pitied.

She'd stayed in the marriage for five long years, determined not to be a failure, and certain she and Billy could work out their problems. Until she discovered a deceit too cruel to ignore. A deceit she could neither forgive nor forget.

But most of all, she was ashamed of deceiving everyone about her baby's father. Especially Cole.

"Oh, honey, I'm sorry. I didn't mean to make you cry," Charlotte said as she rubbed Lauren's shoulder in soothing circles.

Lauren dabbed at her eyes with a tissue and attempted to make light of her tears. "It's not your fault I'm a hormonal mess."

"That's to be expected during pregnancy. Your hormones go whacko."

"Is that your medical diagnosis, Nurse Saunders? Whacko Hormone Syndrome?"

Charlotte chuckled. "It works for me. It's okay to cry, honey. You've been through a lot these last few months. But things are going to get better for you. I can feel it."

Lauren nodded silently. *From your lips to God's*

ears. She prayed Charlotte was right about that rosy future.

Her baby deserved one.

Chapter Five

November 9

The next day, Lauren arrived at the Masonville Veterinary Clinic before eight a.m. Her morning sickness was beginning to wane as she entered her second trimester of pregnancy, but to head off any lingering nausea, she'd nibbled a dry saltine cracker before she lifted her head from her pillow. The last thing she wanted to do on her first day at her new job was to spend the morning throwing up in the bathroom.

Cole's truck was already in the parking lot by the time she arrived. She entered the building and found him waiting for her behind the front reception desk. He smiled and got to his feet as soon as he saw her.

"Hi. How are you this morning?" he asked. He was wearing a lab coat over jeans and a black-and-red-checked flannel shirt. His dark hair shone under the fluorescent lights. Funny, she'd never noticed before how glossy his hair was.

"I'm well, thank you." The smell in the clinic wasn't unpleasant exactly, but there was a distinctive combination of disinfectant and *Eau de Wet Canine* in the air that made her stomach sit up and pay attention. She made herself smile for him. "And ready to start work."

"Good for you. I don't know much about what the

receptionist does, but I had Suzy make a few notes before she left." He handed her a notebook. "She recorded computer passwords, instructions for using the telephone system and the computerized appointments software, and a list of duties she was responsible for."

Lauren thumbed through the slender notebook. Less than a quarter of the pages had been filled. "This is it? This is all she wrote?"

"From what I can gather, Suzy spent a lot of time on the phone handling appointments and dealing with clients and their pets. That's about all I know." He frowned. "I'm sorry to throw you into this without anyone to train you, or any real instructions."

"Don't worry about it. I'll study Suzy's notes, and after that I guess I'll wing it."

He looked slightly horrified, which made her smile. "Don't worry, Cole. I've worked as a receptionist before, and I think your phone system is much the same as one I'm familiar with."

The phone rang, and she grinned at him. "I guess we'll find out right now how much I can improvise."

She punched line one. "Good morning, Masonville Veterinary Clinic. How can I help you?"

"I'd like to make an appointment to get my dog neutered."

"Of course." She booted up the computer using a password she found in Suzy's notebook. "What's your name, sir?"

"Amos Grand."

"Would you like the first available appointment, Mr. Grand, or do you have a specific date in mind?"

"The sooner we get this rascal fixed the better. Given half a chance, he'd spread his seed over the whole state."

Lauren chuckled as she opened the appointment program, and tried to figure out how to use it. "What's this rascal's name?"

"Charlie."

"Let's get Charlie in as soon as possible." She found the search function, typed in Mr. Grand's name, and brought up his file. "Which vet do you usually see?"

"Dr. Waverly."

She managed to open Dr. Waverly's appointment calendar, and she flipped through his schedule. Types of appointments were color-coded—regular check-ups in blue, surgery in pink, and so on. "It looks like Dr. Waverly has an opening for a surgical appointment a week from Friday at eight a.m. Will that work for you?"

"Sounds fine."

"Good." After making sure the contact information was still the same, she typed in Mr. Grand's name, and Charlie's, in the appropriate boxes. "I think that's everything. So next Friday at eight a.m., Mr. Grand."

"Thank you, dearie."

"I'll see you and Charlie then. Goodbye."

"Goodbye, dearie."

She hung up the phone and glanced at Cole. He was smiling as if he were proud of her. Her heart constricted suddenly. Until that moment, she hadn't realized how much his approval meant to her.

"I guess I don't have to worry about you," he said with a wry grin. "You did great."

"Thank you. I appreciate your saying that."

Their gazes locked, and his warm regard touched her like a caress. She was transported to the evening they'd made love in the pasture, and once more she experienced the sensation of being cherished.

The outside vestibule door opened as another staff member arrived. Cole looked away and the moment passed.

Lauren sighed. Cole was her friend. They'd both been grieving and in shock that night. She shouldn't read more into his feelings than what was there.

"Good morning!" A forty-something woman wearing a puffy winter coat breezed through the door. "You must be Lauren. I'm Audrey Johnson. I'm one of the veterinary technicians here at the clinic."

Lauren came around the front desk and extended her hand. "It's nice to meet you, Audrey."

Her grip was firm and friendly. "Nice to meet you, too."

"Audrey, could you introduce Lauren to the rest of the staff? I've got a call this morning."

"Sure, my pleasure."

"Have a good first day, Lauren. I'll be back in the office later this afternoon."

"Do we have your cell phone number in case we need to reach you?"

Before he could answer, Audrey moved behind the desk and pointed at a sheet of paper pinned to a cork board. "His number is here, along with the cell phone numbers of the other two vets."

"Great. Thanks, Audrey."

"No problem. I'm going to put away my coat, but I'll be back in a couple of minutes to introduce you to the others as they arrive. After that, I'll show you around the clinic."

"I appreciate your help."

With a wave, Audrey headed down the hallway. Lauren turned her attention back to Cole. "Don't you have an appointment you have to get to?"

"Yeah, but I…" He shook his head. "I feel like I'm abandoning you."

"You're not. I'll be fine. I'll probably make some mistakes today, but it'll all work out. I'm kind of an expert on first days at work. I've had quite a few."

"Yeah, I guess you have." He ran a hand through his dark hair, mussing it up. "If you need me, phone. You have my number."

"Okay." She'd never bother him with her petty problems while he was on a call, but if it made him feel better to know she could reach him, she'd risk telling the little white lie.

"I should go." Still he didn't leave. "I'm glad you're here, Lauren."

She smiled. "So am I. Now go."

He gave her a salute as he walked backwards out of the reception area. "Aye, aye, Captain."

The crooked smile he aimed at her as he left the reception desk made her laugh. His smile had always been so genuine, so *real.* If Cole smiled she could be sure it meant he was happy or pleased about something. She'd always had to guess what one of Billy's smiles meant. Some of the cruelest words he'd ever said to her were delivered with the sweetest smile.

Wearing pink scrubs emblazoned with cartoon depictions of puppies and kittens, Audrey returned to the reception area at the same time two women arrived through the front door. The older woman wore dark gray scrubs beneath her winter coat, her graying brown hair held back in a ponytail. The younger woman's long, blonde hair hung loose around her shoulders. Since Masonville wasn't a big city, Lauren wasn't surprised that she recognized both women. But in the case of the blonde, it wasn't a pleasant discovery.

"Perfect timing," Audrey said. "Lauren, this is Evelyn Shanks, our kennel attendant. She keeps everything spic and span around here."

Lauren shook her hand. "Hi, Evelyn. It's nice to see you again. I'm not sure if you remember me, but years ago, back in high school, I worked part-time at the hardware store, and you were working there, too."

"Yes, of course I remember you. Welcome to the veterinary clinic. I'm sure you'll like it here."

"Thank you," Lauren said with a smile.

Audrey gestured to the other woman. "And Mia Cottrell is a veterinary technician like me."

"Nice to see you again, Mia," Lauren said, extending her hand to her.

"Yeah." Mia took her hand in a perfunctory shake, her expression less than friendly. "I heard you got the job."

Her tone suggested she didn't agree with the decision to hire her. Lauren ignored her and turned to Evelyn. "How long have you been working here?"

"About five years now. Lauren, I have to tell you how sorry I am about your husband. I'm a big hockey fan, and naturally I followed Billy's career. Hometown boy and all, you know."

"Thank you." Lauren averted her gaze. Accepting condolences for the husband for whom she no longer mourned made her feel phony and totally undeserving of sympathy.

"I'm going to show Lauren around the clinic,"

Audrey said. "Mia, can you carry on with the drug inventory we started yesterday? I'll be there to assist you in a little while."

Mia rolled her eyes. "Fine."

She turned on her heel and left. Audrey sighed.

"Don't pay any attention to Mia. She's a little…difficult."

Evelyn snorted. "Is that what we're calling it now? More like plain old bitchy, I'd say. How do you know her, Lauren?"

"We went to high school together."

"I'm guessing you two weren't exactly bosom buddies back then. Looks like she's still angry with you about something." She lowered her voice. "If there's one thing I've learned about Mia, it's that she can hold a grudge a very long time."

That gave Lauren pause. In her second year at college, Billy dumped Mia to date her again. They married soon after, when they found out Lauren was pregnant. But that was over five years ago. For God's sake, they weren't in college anymore. Mia couldn't possibly still be angry about that.

Could she?

Dr. Waverly and a young woman Lauren recognized from the diner walked into the clinic together. Dr. Waverly held out his hand to her.

"Good to see you, Lauren! We're very happy to have you here."

"Thank you. I'm happy to be here."

"Have you met Jamie? Lauren Walsh, this is Dr. Jamie Garven. She treats companion animals and has an interest in exotics, such as birds and reptiles."

"Reptiles?" Lauren couldn't suppress a tiny

shudder at the thought of snakes and tarantulas. Good grief, did people bring such animals into the clinic?

Jamie laughed. “I saw that wince of horror. Not to worry. I promise I won’t make you handle any reptiles.”

Lauren liked her immediately. “Thank you. That makes me feel a whole lot better.”

Once Jamie and Dr. Waverly left to start their work day, Audrey showed her around the building. They toured the small animal examination rooms, the surgery, the employee break room, and the storage room, where drugs and other supplies such as pet food and supplements for sale were locked away. She led her to a separate building behind the main clinic, connected by a corridor, where large farm animals were brought in and treated. Instead of treatment rooms there were pens, and the surgical suite was larger, with larger equipment such as a portable surgical table, x-ray and ultrasound machines, chutes to confine the animals for treatment, and lifts for moving them around while they were under anesthesia.

“We’re a mixed animal clinic here,” Audrey said. “Like Dr. Waverly said, Jamie primarily deals with companion animals—dogs, cats, and of course exotics. Dr. Waverly used to treat both large and small animals, but since Cole arrived, he’s been cutting back, and mostly works with companion animals here in the clinic, though he will consult on large animal cases occasionally. Cole handles all our large animal calls—cattle, horses, and sometimes hogs, sheep, and goats. Sometimes animals are brought here, but more often Cole goes out to the farms. If it’s a big job, like vaccinating a whole herd, for example, Mia or I will go with him. But he's often out there alone."

A ripple of unease passed through Lauren's body at the thought of Mia working alone with Cole. She shook away the feeling. She was being ridiculous. Cole could have a relationship with anyone he wanted. It wasn't any of her business.

Still…

The tour concluded, they returned to the front reception desk. Audrey turned to her with a friendly smile.

"If you need anything, don't be afraid to give me a holler."

"Thank you. I'm sure I'll have plenty of questions for you in the next few days."

"Good. Can you tell me what time the first appointment of the day arrives?"

Lauren opened the appointment calendar, and after clicking a couple of drop-down menus, she had the answer. "Looks like Jeff Chambers is coming in with his black Lab Winnie at eight-thirty to see Dr. Garven. He's bringing her in because she's been vomiting."

"Nice job!" Audrey gave her an appreciative nod. She checked her watch. "They'll be here any minute. Can you call me as soon as they arrive?"

"Sure."

"Good." She turned to leave, stopped, and turned back again, her voice hushed. "Don't let Mia get you down."

"I won't."

"That's the spirit." She walked down the hallway and entered one of the treatment rooms.

Lauren sighed. Mia's barely suppressed animosity was a pain, but she had more pressing things to worry about. With any luck, she'd come around. They'd never be friends, but she hoped they could at least work together without rancor.

Hopefully, that wasn't too much to ask.

****

Cole skipped lunch in order to get through his appointments as quickly as possible. When his stomach demanded to be fed, he snacked on a protein bar of indeterminate age, found in the glove compartment of his truck. He needed to get back to the clinic to make sure Lauren was okay. Despite her assurances and the knowledge that she was a smart, capable woman, he wanted to check on her himself. She was pregnant. He couldn't allow her to get tired or overwhelmed.

He needn't have worried. On his return, he found her scratching the ears of a golden retriever while chatting amiably with the owner about the cold weather that had suddenly descended upon Masonville. Cole watched her unobserved for a few moments. Her interest in the client and his dog was genuine. Lauren wasn't the kind of person who faked anything.

Perhaps that was one of the reasons he loved her so much.

A moment later the client left and she noticed him watching her. A smile spread over her face, and its warmth wrapped around him. It was stupid to react to her every expression with such intensity. He shouldn't read too much into it. Lauren smiled at everyone. It meant nothing.

How he wished it did.

"Hey, you're back earlier than you expected."

"Yeah." He decided to go with the truth. "I wanted to make sure you were okay."

Her gaze softened. “I told you not to worry. I managed to stumble my way through the day perfectly fine. But thank you for being concerned.”

“You figured out the computer stuff?”

“Mostly. Fortunately, people were remarkably patient once I confessed it was my first day.”

“That’s good. You look tired.”

“No, I’m fine.” Her gaze slid away from his. He narrowed his eyes, alarm ringing in his head.

“Why don’t I believe that? Come on, Lauren. Spill it. What’s wrong?”

Her face turned pink. “It’s nothing, really. It’s stupid. It’s only that I find the smell in the clinic can be…a little overpowering. I have to duck outside for a breath of fresh air occasionally.”

Cole’s first reaction was to laugh, but he sobered after he realized Lauren was serious. “It’s the disinfectants, I guess. I don’t notice the smell anymore. Is it going to be too much for you?”

“No, of course not,” she said quickly. “I’ll get used to it. Since I’ve been pregnant, I’ve been extra sensitive to smells. I’m hoping it’s a phase I’m going through, like the morning sickness.” She shrugged. “At least I didn’t throw up.”

“You’ve had morning sickness?”

“A little,” she said defensively. “It’s not a big deal. Morning sickness is a pretty common symptom of pregnancy in the first few months. And it’s getting better now.”

He’d failed her. Realistically, he could do little to keep her from throwing up in the mornings. But he hadn’t been there for her while she coped with what her body was going through. He’d been so focused on his guilt for taking advantage of her that he'd all but abandoned her. It didn't matter that he'd only found out she was pregnant a few days ago. He'd let her cope with everything by herself.

He wasn't going to make that mistake again.

"How about we celebrate your first day by hitting the Homestead for dinner later?"

"I've got a better idea," she said. "Why don't I cook us dinner? It's the least I can do after you helped me get this job. Besides, you know I love to cook."

He grinned, remembering how she'd experimented with cooking back in high school. Some of her efforts were less than successful—he recalled oatmeal cookies with the consistency of hockey pucks. But she persevered, and by the time he'd left home to go to college, she'd become a pretty passable cook.

"Okay, but only if I can help. You've had a long day."

"All right, you're on. Charlotte's house after work."

The fact that she'd agreed to let him help told him that she was more tired than she'd admit. He'd damn well look after her whether she wanted him to or not.

"I'll be there."

****

A couple of hours later Cole arrived at Lauren's sister's house carrying a box of chocolates that he'd picked up at the Masonville drugstore. He hoped the pregnancy hadn't affected her sweet tooth.

She spied the box as soon as she opened the door. He suppressed a laugh at the look of rapture on her face.

She didn't bother to say hello as she grabbed his

arm and pulled him inside. "Please tell me that's a box of Gibbon's hand-dipped chocolates you've got in your hand."

"And I was worried you wouldn't like them anymore."

"Are you kidding? I've had dreams about those chocolates, especially since I've been pregnant. You can't imagine the cravings I've had." She tore her gaze away from the box to look into his eyes. "I'm surprised you remembered."

He remembered everything about Lauren. He'd given her a box of the chocolates on one of their movie dates back in high school. The date hadn't been a big hit, but the chocolates certainly had been. Cole could still remember the look of bliss on her face as she bit into one of the chocolates for the first time. Her eyelids had slowly fluttered shut as her lips closed around the sour cherry covered with dark chocolate. It had been the most sensual, erotic thing he'd ever seen—until he'd seen her face the day they'd made love. His groin tightened at the thought, and he shifted uncomfortably.

Handing the box to her, he unzipped his coat and slid it off his shoulders. Charlotte's dog danced around him as he hung it in the closet by the front door. He scratched Daisy's ears.

"How could I forget? You practically drooled on me the last time I gave you some of these. Think of the chocolates as a 'congratulations for making it through your first day of work' present."

She laughed. "Thank you. It was very thoughtful of you. Come on into the kitchen."

Cole followed her and Daisy through the small living room and even smaller dining room. He noticed that she'd set the dining room table for two.

"Isn't Charlotte home?" he asked.

"She's working till midnight tonight."

Visions of an intimate, candlelit dinner for two ending with dessert in her bedroom raced through his head, but he quelled the image. He had to keep his emotions, and his libido, under control. If Lauren guessed the direction of his thoughts, and his feelings for her, the evening would be over before it began.

Besides, there was nothing remotely romantic about the way she'd set the table. No candles, no flowers, no fancy glassware. Just serviceable, everyday dishes that got the job done.

Sort of like me. His brother had been the exciting one, thrilling women with his daring athleticism. He was simply a guy who went to work every day and did the best he could. Not exactly exciting, and certainly not romantic.

They entered the kitchen, and Lauren handed him a paring knife. "You said you'd help, right?"

"Sure. What do you want me to do?"

"We're having a stir-fry. Could you help me chop some vegetables?"

"Of course."

He washed his hands at the kitchen sink before chopping onions and carrots on the cutting board she'd given him. Lauren worked beside him at the sink, washing lettuce and other vegetables for a salad.

"So tell me about your first day. Aside from the smell, did everything go okay?"

She wrinkled her nose. "I wish I hadn't told you that. Now you're going to obsess over it."

"No, I'm not. But I might get some sort of air

freshener for the reception area. You're probably not the only person who finds the clinic a little strong-smelling." He chopped the bunch of green onions she handed him. "Were you able to figure out the appointment system on the computer?"

"Yes, mostly. It's reasonably user friendly. I'm sure I'll get a lot more proficient with it in the next few weeks." She kept her gaze focused on the lettuce she rinsed under the tap. "It's important to me to do a good job."

"I told you before, I have no doubt you'll be great at the job."

She looked up at him. "You're a good friend, Cole."

The tender look in her eyes made him want to pull her close and kiss her until they were both shaking with need. Instead he looked away and sliced mushrooms into uneven chunks, unnerved by the way his hands trembled. Friendship was the only thing she wanted from him, so that's what he'd give her.

"Hurry it along with the food, would you? I'm starved." He didn't have to fake the gruffness in his voice.

She laughed. "Okay, okay. Has anyone ever told you you're grumpy when you're hungry?"

"Everyone's told me that."

Lauren heated a wok and cooked pieces of sliced chicken before adding vegetables and seasonings. She tossed the salad with an olive oil and balsamic vinegar dressing, and after arranging the stir-fry on a plate with brown rice, she brought both dishes to the table.

"*Bon appétit*," she said.

They ate in compatible silence for a while. Cole

sipped on his water, and leaned back in his chair.

"This is really good."

"Thanks. I'm trying to eat healthy, for the baby. Lots of veggies and fruit, and not too much junk food. Though you're making it really hard to be good by giving me those chocolates."

"I could take them home with me if you don't want to be tempted," he teased.

"Don't you dare!" she said with a laugh. She dabbed at her mouth with her napkin, her smile disappearing. "I'll do whatever I can to have a healthy baby. This child is very important to me. I miscarried twice before."

He put down his fork and reached for her hand. He'd known about the first miscarriage because his mother had bitterly complained about how Lauren had trapped Billy into marriage with a pregnancy and then promptly lost the baby. But he hadn't known there'd been a second loss. "You never told me. What happened?"

"They tell me it's nature's way of weeding out a non-viable fetus. But for me, it wasn't so clinical. It was the death of a child, even if I was only twelve weeks pregnant."

"But you're farther along now. If you're due in March, you must be over sixteen weeks pregnant."

She gave him a bleak, anguished look before quickly averting her gaze. "Yes. Sixteen weeks."

He squeezed her hand. "Hey, it's going to be okay. You're going to eat all your veggies and deliver a healthy, happy baby. I promise."

"You promise?" A hint of a smile curved her lips.

"I promise."

He couldn't guarantee anything. But he wanted her to believe things would be okay this time.

"All right."

"Good. Eat your greens."

She chuckled as she picked up her fork and began eating again.

By the time they finished dinner, it was past eight p.m. and Cole saw the fatigue on her face. It had been a long day for her, and she had to be exhausted. He grabbed her hand and led her out of the kitchen.

"What are you doing?" she said. "I have to clean up."

"You cooked, so I'll clean."

He brought her to the living room, where he found an afghan draped over the arm of the sofa. He picked it up and placed it around her shoulders.

"Lie down for a while and rest. I'll take care of the dishes."

"But—"

"No buts. Lie down."

She frowned, but did as he ordered. "When did you get so bossy?"

When I found out you were pregnant. "You never noticed before?"

"Strangely, no. I used to think you were so mild mannered."

He tucked the afghan around her and handed her the TV remote. "Maybe you haven't been paying attention all these years."

Their gazes locked. It took Cole a second to realize what he'd said. She hadn't paid attention to him, at least not in the way he'd wanted her to. Now that Billy was gone, would things change?

He didn't want to be her second choice. He didn't want her to settle for him because she could no longer have the man she loved.

He swallowed and looked away. "It won't take me long to clean up. Stay where you are."

She said nothing as he left the room. He washed up the few dishes he couldn't get into the dishwasher, then wiped the counters, putting everything in order in about fifteen minutes.

The sound of the TV drifted in from the living room. He hesitated before joining her in the other room, needing to put on the mask he wore around her, the one that concealed his true feelings for her. Making sure there was a bland expression on his face, he left the kitchen.

He found Lauren sound asleep with the dog curled at her feet, the remote still in her hand. Cole gently pried it from her fingers and turned off the TV. Kneeling beside the sofa, he looked into her face. She looked peaceful, almost angelic. He smiled to himself, imagining how she'd roll her eyes if he told her she looked like an angel. She'd never understood how beautiful she was.

He touched the sweet curve of her cheek with a gentle caress, careful not to wake her. Her skin was petal soft and fragrant, with a scent of vanilla that filled his senses. He loved her. He ached with loving her.

He laid his hand on the soft swell of her belly. He loved her baby too, because it was a part of her. It didn't matter that it was his brother's child.

He watched her sleep for several long minutes before finally pushing himself to a standing position and making himself walk out the door.

Chapter Six

November 22

"We have Lucy's appointment set up for two p.m. next Tuesday with Dr. Waverly. I'll see you then, Mrs. Smith."

"Wonderful. Thank you, Lauren."

Lauren hung up the phone and went back to her accounting program. She'd been at the clinic for two weeks and things were falling into place. She enjoyed meeting the pets of Masonville and its surrounding area, and she loved the quick pace of the clinic. Dr. Waverly had handed over the responsibility of the daily accounting to her, and she was happy to be using her skills and thrilled to be treated like a trusted, valuable employee. For the first time in a long time she really *belonged.* Except for a couple of irritants, the job would be perfect.

A few times she'd noticed that the cash drawer was out of balance with the receipts recorded in the accounting system. The cash shortages were small, only five or ten dollars at a time. At first, she thought she'd made an error in giving out change, and she'd replaced the money herself. But after the third time, she realized there was more going on than a simple mistake. She mentioned the discrepancy to Dr. Waverly and he expressed surprise but said there had to be a logical explanation. Lauren believed so too—someone was helping themselves. But she had no proof of anything. According to Dr. Waverly, they'd never had problems with cash shortages in the past, which led her to believe they began at the same time she started working at the clinic. Dr. Waverly didn't appear concerned right now, but if they continued, she was afraid he'd come to believe she was responsible for the thefts. The thought unsettled her. She couldn't afford to lose this job, and even more importantly, she couldn't afford to lose her reputation. Who would hire an accountant who was accused of stealing money?

Mia Cottrell entered the reception area and walked around the front desk to stand next to her, her expression oozing phony concern. "Lauren, are you feeling okay? You look a little…puffy."

And the second irritant just walked in.

Lauren bit back a pithy reply. Since the day she'd started work at the clinic, Mia had taken every opportunity to make snide comments about her appearance and the fact that she was gaining weight. She was careful to confront her while no one else was around, like now. Mia's comments were usually veiled in a guise of caring, but that didn't fool Lauren for a moment. She was trying to undermine her confidence, make her feel unattractive.

It was working.

She pasted a smile on her face. "I'm fine, but thank you for your concern."

"You look so tired. Such bags under your eyes. Have you not been sleeping?"

She resisted the urge to touch a finger to her eye to test the puffiness. "I'm sleeping like a baby."

"How is the baby? I'm worried about you. I know you've lost two pregnancies before..." She let the statement hang in the air.

Lauren twisted in her chair to look at her, a sick feeling in her stomach. "How did you know that?"

Mia gave her a look of wide-eyed innocence. "Your sister Charlotte must have told me."

Like hell she did. Charlotte hadn't spoken to Mia since she caught her necking with her boyfriend at the senior prom.

"Try again."

"I guess Billy must have told me. We...chatted from time to time."

It hurt to know that Billy had spoken to Mia about the saddest, most gut-wrenching experiences of her life. Lauren turned away, not wanting her to see how much her words affected her.

"Thank you for your concern. The baby and I are fine."

"That's good. I'd hate to think something bad would happen again. It would be such a shame if you were to lose *Billy's* baby."

The emphasis Mia placed on Billy's name made Lauren look up sharply. Did she guess the baby wasn't her husband's? Exactly how close had she been to Billy in recent years?

Audrey walked into the reception area leading a pug on her leash, the dog's owner right behind her.

"Lauren, could you get Mrs. Martin's invoice ready? Mia, grab a bag of the weight control dog food formula from the storage room, please."

"Yes, of course." Lauren managed a pleasant smile for her customer. She was disconcerted to discover that her fingers trembled as she tried to work the keyboard. Out of the corner of her eye, she saw Mia give Audrey an angry glare before going into the back room for the dog food.

As soon as the customer paid her bill and left with her dog and its supplies, Audrey turned to Mia, one eyebrow raised.

"Don't you have an inventory to finish? I'm sure Lauren has work to do."

"Fine." Mia gave Lauren one last disdainful smirk before turning on her heel and leaving the reception area. Lauren closed her eyes and blew out her breath, pushing back the tears that were so close to the surface. *Everything* made her emotional these days. Forget about watching the news. Any hint of children in trouble, of death and destruction anywhere in the world, caused her to have a minor breakdown. Even commercials made her cry.

"Don't pay any attention to Mia. She's jealous," Audrey said quietly.

That was a surprise. "Jealous? Of me?"

"Yes, you. She has designs on Cole, but she sees the way he looks at you. She thinks of you as a threat."

"That's ridiculous. I'm not a threat to anyone. And Cole and I are old friends. He doesn't look at me any differently than any other woman."

"Maybe you should pay more attention." Audrey laid her hand on Lauren's arm. "I know you recently lost your husband, and you may not be ready for a new relationship, but a man like Cole doesn't come along every day. He seems to genuinely care for you."

"We've been friends since we were kids." That's all it was, wasn't it? Friendship? "He's a very kind person."

"Yes, he is." Audrey patted her arm.

A new client arrived for an appointment with Dr. Jamie, and Audrey ushered him and his dog into an examining room. Lauren went back to her accounting program, but the numbers swam before her eyes. Did Cole look at her differently than he did other women?

She hoped Audrey was wrong about Mia having designs on Cole. The thought of the two of them together made her feel unsettled and edgy, and a little nauseated.

Are you jealous, Lauren?

She squirmed in her chair. She wasn't jealous. It was only that Mia was so wrong for Cole. She'd chew him up and spit him out without a backward glance. Cole deserved someone who really loved him.

Yes, that had to be what she was feeling. Concern for her friend.

But as the day continued, her unsettled mood persisted. The idea of Cole being with someone else, even someone who wasn't Mia, burned a trail of jealousy in her gut.

****

Cole was happy to be spending the day at the clinic for a change. One of his clients was bringing in his goats for vaccination in the morning, and the rest of the day he'd be helping Jamie with companion animal appointments since Dr. Waverly was away for a couple of days. He didn't get a lot of time to be close to Lauren, so he was glad for the opportunity.

But he knew something was wrong the minute he returned from the large animal clinic where he'd been working with the goats. Lauren was pale and subdued.

As Seth Paxton, the owner of the goats, paid his bill, she barely said a word, totally unlike her normal friendly self. She'd been at the clinic nearly a month, and whenever he'd been in the clinic, he'd seen her chatting with clients and asking questions about the care and feeding and temperament of their pets, especially some of the more exotic animals that Jamie specialized in treating.

Cole's gut twisted. Something was wrong.

As soon as Seth left the building, he cleared his throat.

"Lauren, can I speak to you for a moment? In examining room three?"

She blinked at him, obviously surprised by his request. He caught a look of worry in her eyes as well. "Yes, of course."

She got to her feet and followed him into the examining room. Cole closed the door.

"Is everything all right?"

She swallowed and looked away. "Yes, of course."

He touched her shoulder and tried to look into her face. "You're very quiet today."

"I guess I'm tired."

"Why don't you go home and lie down for a while?"

"I can't do that. It's not even noon. I've got work to do."

"Lauren." Gently grasping her chin, he tipped it upward, forcing her to look at him. "Let me help. Tell me what's wrong."

She closed her eyes and a tear slid down her cheek.

"I'm afraid I'm losing the baby," she whispered.

His gut clenched. She'd be devastated if anything

happened to this baby. "What's going on?"

"I started spotting this morning after I got to work. That's what happened the last couple of times, before I miscarried." Her breath hitched. "I'm scared, Cole."

He pulled her into his arms and held her tightly, needing to protect her and the baby. She clung to him, her arms locked around his waist. "It's going to be okay, sweetheart. Who's your doctor?"

"Grant McKenzie."

"I'm going to call him right now, okay? He'll know what to do."

She lifted her head from his chest to look up at him. Her face was streaked with tears, her expression bleak, as if she expected the worst.

"Okay," she said. She sat on one of the chairs next to the examining table, her head bowed in resignation. As if she expected the worst.

He pulled his phone from his pocket and did a quick search for the phone number of the Masonville Family Health Clinic. A moment later he had Grant McKenzie's nurse on the line.

"I'm calling for Lauren Walsh. She's a patient of Dr. McKenzie's. She's about twenty weeks pregnant and experiencing some spotting that we're concerned about. I'd like to speak to the doctor."

"Please hold for a moment."

Several seconds ticked by. Cole paced the small room, his impatience growing with every step. Dammit, what was taking so long? Realistically, he understood the doctor was busy. He probably had several patients clamoring for his attention. But he didn't give a damn about any of the doctor's other patients. Lauren was the only one he cared about, and she needed his help. Now.

Finally, there was a click and someone picked up. "Grant McKenzie here."

"Dr. McKenzie, Cole Walsh. I'm calling for my sister-in-law, Lauren Walsh."

"My nurse says she's been spotting."

"Yes."

"Can you bring her in to my office? I can see her right away."

"Yes, of course. We can be there in about ten minutes."

Lauren was silent all the way to the doctor's office. As soon as they arrived, the nurse led her into one of the examining rooms. He wanted to go with her, to support her, to hold her hand if nothing else. But he was only her brother-in-law, not her husband. He had no right to be with her.

The thought filled him with desolation. He'd never have the right to be with her.

He sent text messages to Jamie and Audrey, telling them what was going on. He paced the waiting room and counted the number of steps needed to circle the room. He tried reading one of the months-old magazines, but he couldn't concentrate on the words. All he could think about was Lauren lying on an examining table, scared and alone. He ached to be with her.

"Dr. Walsh?" Dr. McKenzie's nurse entered the waiting room. "Lauren is asking for you. Can you come with me?"

"Yes, of course."

He followed her through a labyrinth of hallways to a room at the back. Lauren looked up as he entered the room. She was dressed in her street clothes, sitting in front of a large desk. Cole sat next to her and reached for her hands, holding them tightly.

"Dr. McKenzie will be in to see you in a couple of minutes." The nurse closed the door, leaving them alone.

"What has he told you?" Cole asked.

"Nothing yet. He examined me, did some tests. I'm waiting for the results." She bowed her head. "I asked the nurse to call you because I didn't want to be alone. If Dr. McKenzie is going to tell me that I'm losing this baby… The last time I miscarried, I was by myself. It was scary. There was a lot of blood…"

Christ. "You're not alone, sweetheart. I'm right here."

She smiled weakly. "Thank you."

Dr. McKenzie stepped inside the office. Lauren gripped Cole's hands a little tighter.

"I'm sorry to keep you waiting, but the news is good. It doesn't appear as if you're in imminent danger of losing the pregnancy."

She released a breath on a sob. "You're sure?"

"There are no guarantees, but the baby's heartbeat is strong, your hormone levels are rising the way we would expect them to, and your cervix is still closed. Those are all good indicators that everything is progressing normally."

"But the spotting? What does that mean?"

"Spotting usually occurs earlier in a pregnancy, but it's not unheard of at sixteen weeks. Sometimes it doesn't mean anything."

"Sixteen weeks?" Cole said. "You mean twenty weeks, don't you? Lauren is due in March."

The doctor picked up Lauren's file and looked

through his notes. "Lauren was quite clear about her dates. She's sixteen weeks pregnant with a due date of April twenty-second. The size of the fetus is consistent with that date."

Cole's head started to spin. Did this mean…

"I think you should stay off your feet for a day or two, Lauren," the doctor said. "If you have any cramping, or if the spotting increases or turns bright red, I want you to call me right away. Okay?"

"Okay."

He looked from Lauren to Cole and back again. "If you need to talk, about anything, call me."

She swallowed. "I will. Thank you, Doctor McKenzie."

They left the office together, neither of them speaking. Cole couldn't form words, couldn't think. He'd known there was a possibility he'd fathered her child, but he believed the chances were remote, especially given her supposed due date. In the parking lot he helped Lauren into his truck before getting behind the wheel himself. He put the truck into gear and drove, but instead of taking her to her sister's house, he found himself on the highway, heading out of town.

Beside him, Lauren said nothing, though he could feel the nervous glances she threw his way. He drove until he found the turnoff that took them to the back road leading to the pasture. To their secret place. Pulling to a stop in front of the barbed wire fence, he killed the engine. His thoughts flew in a thousand directions as he stared unseeing out the windshield.

"Is the baby mine?" he said finally.

She sighed out a long breath. "Yes."

"You're sure it's not Billy's?"

"I'm sure. Billy and I hadn't…we hadn't been together for a while before his death."

"Could someone else be the father?"

"No! Of course not! I've never been with anyone besides Billy."

He turned to look at her, frustration building inside him. "And me."

"Yes. And you," she whispered.

"Were you ever going to tell me?" He struggled to keep the anger out of his voice.

"I wanted to tell you as soon as I found out. I called the clinic, but you were out of town, and then everyone found out and assumed the baby was Billy's. I was too much of a coward to tell them they were wrong. And I didn't know how you'd feel about the news. It's not like you signed up to be a father. I threw myself at you without being smart enough to even consider birth control. I'm sorry, Cole. You deserved to know the truth from the start."

Cole stared out the windshield once more. Emotions tripped over themselves inside his head. Anger and frustration eventually gave way to understanding. She'd been put in a terrible position. How could she explain—to her family, his mother, and the small town that thought of Billy as a hero—that she'd slept with him on the day of her husband's funeral? He only wished she could have trusted him enough to tell him the truth.

I'm going to be a father. The thought sparkled brightly in his mind. He was going to have a child with Lauren, the woman he loved.

"You didn't throw yourself at me. You were

hurting."

"So were you. You'd just buried your brother."

Cole turned to her and reached for her hand. "Neither of us was thinking straight that night. We needed each other, and out of that need a child was conceived. That's the important thing. We have to do what's right for the baby."

"Yes. I agree."

The answer came to Cole in a flash, and he knew exactly what he had to do. "I think the best thing for the baby is to have two parents, a mother and a father. I think we should get married."

Lauren's eyes went wide with shock. "We can't do that!"

"Why not? Neither of us is married or attached. And we have a baby on the way that needs us. I want to be a part of my child's life right from the beginning."

"I understand, Cole, really I do, but how do I tell my family and your mother that you're the father of my child? And what about other people, our coworkers, our friends? What will they think?"

"Do you really care so much what people think? Isn't the welfare of your child more important?"

"Of course it is!" He could see she struggled to hold back tears. "But my family's opinion of me means everything. I couldn't bear to lose their respect. They'd be humiliated if we became the topic of gossip in town. I couldn't do that to them. And your mother! Oh, God, your mother."

He wanted to tell her that, in time, any gossip about them would die down. Eventually the busybodies would find something more interesting to blather about. Their families would get over it, especially once the baby arrived. But she was too distressed to believe anything he said right now, and arguing would likely upset her even more.

He could practically feel her withdrawal, her goodbye. He held tight to her hand, not allowing her to pull away.

"We don't need to tell anyone I'm the baby's father, not if you don't want to. Everyone already believes Billy fathered your child, so let them go on thinking it. As long as you and I know the truth, nothing else matters."

She stared at him. "Is that really what you want?"

No! I want to shout from the rooftops that you're having my baby!

"I'm fine with whatever makes you comfortable."

"Cole, I don't know—"

"Lauren, please. I want to be a part of my child's life. Marry me and help me make a family for our baby. He deserves a family."

"I know he does. Or she."

"Have you thought whether you'd like a boy or a girl?"

She shrugged. "It doesn't matter to me. I know it's a cliché, but I really don't care as long as he or she is healthy."

Cole gently raked one knuckle across her cheek. "I think I'd like a girl. One who looks like you."

Her eyes narrowed, as if she didn't quite trust him. "What kind of marriage are you proposing? Something in name only, something we put on for the neighbors for show? Or are you interested in a real marriage?"

"If by a real marriage you mean one where we live together as husband and wife, we work together, build a family together, and we sleep together, yeah, that's what I want. I'm not interested in putting on a show, Lauren. I'm not going to push myself on you, but I want something real."

She looked away and he saw her struggling for composure once more. "I want something real, too. I won't tolerate any cheating."

His heart broke for her. He knew about his brother's infidelity. Billy had even bragged about some of his affairs. It sickened him to think he'd been so disloyal to Lauren. If she had knowledge of the affairs, she'd chosen to look the other way because she loved Billy so much.

"I won't tolerate cheating either. Once I marry you, you'll be the only woman I'll ever be with again. I promise you that."

She lifted her gaze to his, and Cole saw a flash of pain in her eyes. He squeezed her hands once more. "I promise you, Lauren. I'll be true to you."

A hint of a smile played on her beautiful mouth. "I know. I trust you." Her gaze lowered to their joined hands. "Did you want to get married right away, or wait until after the baby is born?"

He answered without hesitation. "Right away. The sooner the better."

"Maybe you should consider waiting a while."

Her gaze was still on their hands and he couldn't see her eyes to gauge what she was thinking. "Why?"

She lifted her head, but her gaze didn't connect with his. "Because if I lose the baby, you'll have married me for nothing."

His heart constricted. He brought her hands to his mouth and tenderly kissed each one.

"First of all, you're not going to lose the baby. Dr. McKenzie said everything looks as it should. You're going to spend a couple of days resting, and everything's going to be fine. Okay?"

Her hopeful expression told him she wanted to believe him. "Okay."

"Secondly, even if the worst happens it wouldn't change my mind. I'd still want to marry you."

She blinked at him, surprised. It was the closest he'd ever come to telling her what was in his heart. Her mouth opened as if she was about to say something, but instead she closed it and stared into his eyes. He wondered if she could hear the chaotic thoughts rolling around in his brain. After several long moments, she expelled a deep, shaky breath.

"You're sure this is what you want?"

"I'm absolutely sure." He tamped down the elation rising in his heart, not wanting to reveal his eagerness.

"Then I guess I'm saying yes, I'll marry you."

He pulled her towards him and rested his forehead against hers. "I'll make you happy, Lauren. I promise."

His heart sang in joy. He loved her and he'd wanted her for a long time. He meant what he said. He'd spend the rest of his life doing everything he could to make her happy.

He tried not to dwell on the fact that she hadn't actually said she wanted to marry him too, only that she would.

Chapter Seven

November 23

Lauren's spotting stopped the next day. Her grateful heart filled with hope once more. Maybe this time she would hold a baby in her arms.

She would have gone back to work, but Cole insisted she stay home and rest at least one more day.

Cole. She couldn't quite believe she was marrying him. But she was, and somehow it made sense. He was marrying her because she was pregnant, but she believed his claim that he'd want to marry her even if she lost the baby. Of everything he'd said, those were the words that convinced her to say yes.

But that didn't mean she wasn't scared. After the debacle of her first marriage, she had to be cautious. Her child deserved the best chance in life.

Cole deserved the best, too, and he also deserved to be happy. She wished she could believe she was the woman who could give him everything he wanted.

They'd decided to tell their families right away. Cole had called her family and his mother and invited them to his house for the big reveal this evening. As soon as he finished work, he'd pick her up at Charlotte's so they could prepare. Lauren wasn't sure exactly what they were preparing for. Best that the news was delivered quickly and as painlessly as possible, without a prolonged build-up. Her family would be surprised, maybe even shocked, that she planned to marry so quickly after being widowed, but they'd come around. They liked and respected Cole.

But his mother was a different story. Billy had been her everything, her shining star. Lauren suspected Ella wanted her to mourn him forever the way she planned to do.

Cole arrived around five-thirty to pick her up. If Charlotte wondered what was going on, she didn't ask. She simply promised to pick up Ella and bring her to Cole's house around seven.

As soon as Cole opened the door of his house, a golden retriever barked and circled him excitedly, jumping up on him and laying his huge paws on his chest.

"Down, boy. Sit."

The dog jumped down and sat, looking up at Cole with love. Lauren held out her hand so he could sniff it. He licked her fingers affectionately, and she scratched his head.

"He's beautiful, Cole. What's his name?"

"Brady. He's a great dog, but as you can see, not exactly obedient."

"Well, I think he's a sweetheart, aren't you, Brady?"

The dog barked at the sound of his name. He sat at her feet and lifted a paw for her to shake.

"I think you've made a conquest. I'm glad you like him, since you'll soon be living here with us."

Lauren quelled the nervousness in her stomach at the thought. Cole was a dear friend, but living with someone, even someone she cared for deeply, was a challenge. She'd learned that the hard way. Each of them had quirks and idiosyncrasies they'd have to learn to live with on a day-to-day basis. Compromises and allowances had to be made. Brady was one of them. She hadn't had a dog since she was ten years old, and as much as she loved dogs, taking care of one was a little like caring for a toddler. She was going to be a new mother soon; she wasn't sure she could handle Brady as well as an infant.

Cole set his bags of take-out food from the Homestead Restaurant on the dining room table. He gave her an apologetic grin.

"I'm not much of a cook. I thought you'd be safer with take-out."

"Now I know why you're marrying me. You need someone to cook for you."

"That's my evil plan. Marry you, and keep you chained to the stove."

I'd rather be chained to your bed.

She blinked as the words entered her thoughts. An image ripped through her memory. Cole looming over her, looking deeply into her eyes as his body entered hers, both of them hot and slick with sweat. It had been so good, so perfect…

Lauren stumbled on the area carpet in the dining room. Maybe the pregnancy hormones were making her a little crazy.

"You okay?" He reached out a hand to steady her.

"I'm fine, just klutzy."

She'd never had erotic thoughts about Cole before. He was her friend, someone she'd cared about for years, like her friend Megan from college, or Greta, from the Homestead.

Of course, she'd never had sex with Megan or Greta.

Great sex.

Cole removed the food from the bags and set the Styrofoam containers on the table. He'd purchased roast beef sandwiches and a tossed salad with dressing on the side. After bringing plates and cutlery to the table, they helped themselves.

"So do you have a plan of attack for tonight? What exactly are we going to say?"

"We're going to tell the truth."

Lauren put down her sandwich, her appetite evaporating. "The truth?"

"To a point," he clarified. "We'll tell our families we've decided the baby needs a family, a mother and a father. We've been friends for a long time and we feel we'd be compatible."

"Okay, that sounds reasonable." She picked up her sandwich once more and bit into it. "This is delicious," she said once she'd swallowed. "Thanks for not cooking."

"Any time." Cole stabbed at his salad with a fork. "I thought I'd also mention the financial advantages of our marriage. Two steady incomes instead of one, and a house that's paid for. The baby can even have her own room. I can afford to give her things like piano lessons or swimming lessons. Anything she wants."

"Wait a minute." Lauren put down her sandwich again and jumped to her feet. "Is that the real reason you want to marry me? Because you think I can't afford to look after my child?"

To her shame, she teetered on the verge of tears. She'd made the mistake of thinking Cole actually wanted to marry her. But she was fooling herself. If she hadn't been pregnant with his child, he wouldn't have made his offer.

Cole jumped to his feet as well. "That's not what I meant. I know you'd find a way to look after the baby on your own. You're a hard worker, and you're smart. But you shouldn't have to work so hard. This baby is my responsibility, too. It will be easier if both of us share the load. Our families can understand that." He grasped her shoulders with both hands. "This child means everything to me. I want our baby to have everything she needs, and everything she wants. I want her to be happy, and if that means piano lessons, fine. If it means buying her a pony, that's fine, too. Let me be part of my child's life, Lauren. Please."

For the first time it hit Lauren that Cole loved their baby as much as she did. She wouldn't be alone raising this child. Cole would be right beside her, holding her hand. It meant the world to know he cared so much for their child. She only wished his feelings for her went farther.

She shook her head at the incongruity of her thoughts. Her feelings for him hadn't changed. She still thought of him as a friend. A dear, kind friend, whose kiss made her tremble in his arms. But still, a friend. She couldn't ask more of him than he was able to give. And she couldn't ask more of him than she was able to give in return.

She released a shaky breath and sat once more. Cole sat as well.

"I'm sorry. You're right," she said. "Our families would understand us wanting to prepare financially for the baby. It's not like I have a solid career."

"You mentioned in your interview that you want to finish your degree."

"I'd like to. If I finished my degree, I could get an accounting designation which would give me a better chance of getting a good, steady job with decent pay. But it's more of a fantasy wish right now." Finishing her degree would also give her a sense of accomplishment that she sorely needed.

Cole chewed thoughtfully for a moment. "I think you should go for it. Once the baby is born, we'll figure out a way to make it happen."

She stared at him. "You mean it?"

"Of course I do."

Whenever she'd tried to talk to Billy about finishing her degree, he dismissed the idea, saying they didn't have the money for school. Aside from that, Billy was too wrapped up in his own career aspirations to care about hers.

Cole probably didn't understand all the sacrifices they'd both have to make in order for her dream to become a reality. But at least he was willing to consider it.

"Finish your sandwich, Lauren. You need to eat," he said gently.

She picked it up once more, discovering that she was suddenly famished. She polished it off in a few bites.

****

Everyone arrived at his house around seven. As he'd expected, his mother was full of questions the minute she walked through the door.

"What's this all about, Cole? What was so important you had to summon us to your house on a

Thursday evening?"

"I won't keep you in suspense for long, Ma. As soon as Garrett arrives, we'll get started."

"Can I get you some tea, Ella?" Lauren offered.

She huffed out a breath. "Since we have to wait, I suppose we might as well have tea."

Lauren and Charlotte brought a pot of tea and enough tea cups for everyone, along with the cookies Lauren had baked and brought with her. Cole noted that she'd chosen his grandmother's china teacups. He'd never used them before. After his grandmother's death two years ago, he'd inherited the house and everything in it, including the teacups. When she'd informed him she'd changed her will to leave everything she had to him, he'd been stunned, and tried to talk her out of it. But she'd insisted his mother had favored Billy so much over the years that it was time to even things out. Ella had argued with her mother that her estate should be divided equally between the two grandsons, but Elizabeth Morris had held firm. Cole was grateful for her stubbornness. The house was old-fashioned and desperately needed updates, but it was solid and cozy, and able to keep out a cold North Dakota wind.

The inheritance had caused a rift between him and his brother that had never healed. Grandma Morris had been right. Billy had gotten more than his fair share from their parents—more help financially, more attention, more respect.

The thought made him feel disloyal and petty.

Garrett arrived a moment later, knocking on the door before stepping inside. Once Garrett was settled with a cup of tea and a cookie, Cole got to his feet and held out his hand to Lauren. She rose and put her hand in his, holding it tightly as she stood beside him and faced the assembled group.

"We asked you to come here this evening because we have something we want to tell all of you. Lauren and I are getting married."

The room went deathly quiet. Lauren tightened her grip on his hand. Her face turned pale as she stared at her family's stunned expressions. Cole put his arm around her waist, afraid she might faint.

He needn't have worried. She lifted her chin at a defiant angle and turned to face the others.

"Cole and I have decided this child needs the best possible start in life and that means having a mother *and* a father. We've always been friends, so what better way to start a marriage then with friendship?"

Garrett pushed himself to his feet and came forward. "I think it's a hell of an idea. You two will make wonderful parents."

He enfolded Lauren in an embrace. Cole heard her murmur her thanks to her brother. "I think you'll make a wonderful uncle."

Charlotte was next in line. She kissed Lauren's cheek. "I'm so happy for you, sweetie. When's the big day?"

"In a couple of weeks," Cole said. "As soon as we can arrange everything."

Lauren's parents, Robert and Grace, also extended their congratulations. If they had reservations, they kept them to themselves.

Only his mother remained in her seat, staring at them in disbelief.

Cole sat next to her. "What do you want to say, Ma?"

"You can't replace Billy." She choked out the words.

"I know that." He'd known he was second best in her eyes all his life. "I wouldn't even try."

"But to marry his wife, to raise his child? It's wrong. They don't belong to you. You always wanted what belonged to your brother."

He wanted to shout at her that the baby was his, that it had nothing to do with Billy. And Lauren was his, too. He'd loved her first. His brother had never appreciated what a gem he'd had in her. He'd squandered his marriage the way he'd squandered the love that had been lavished on him all his life, from his parents, from Lauren, and even from him.

Instead he pressed his lips together and said nothing. He felt a hand on his shoulder, and saw that Lauren stood beside him.

"I know this is difficult for you, Ella. I know you're grieving. But I have to raise my child in the best way I know how. Aside from my brother and sister, Cole is my best friend in the world. He's a good man, and I know he'll be a wonderful father. You should be very proud of him."

His mother stared at Lauren as if she couldn't believe what she was saying. Her face twisted. "Don't you miss Billy at all? Don't you grieve for him? Nobody understands. Nobody."

"Ma."

He said the word a little sharper then he'd intended, but at least it got her attention. She looked up at him in surprise.

"I'm sorry if it hurts you, but Lauren and I are getting married. We care about one another and we care about the baby. The three of us are going to be a family. I wish you could be happy for us."

Ella dabbed at her eyes with a tissue. Finally, with a shuddering breath, she turned to look at him.

"For Billy's baby's sake, I'll try."

Billy's baby.

The pain was swift and unexpected. If she'd stabbed him through the heart with a dagger it wouldn't have hurt as much. Lauren squeezed his shoulder again, telling him she understood. He covered her hand with his, absorbing her strength.

Grace approached his mother. "Ella, would you like us to drive you home? Robert and I are going right by your apartment."

"Yes, thank you. I think I'd like to leave now."

She got to her feet and brushed past him, not bothering to say goodbye. Grace kissed Lauren, and Robert shook his hand before they ushered his mother from the house. He closed his eyes in relief at her departure. Garrett clapped him on the back.

"I don't know about you, but I could use something stronger than tea. What've you got?"

"Scotch. In the cabinet over the fridge."

"Perfect. Two fingers?"

"Sounds good. No ice."

Garrett left to retrieve the scotch. Lauren sat next to him and reached for his hand.

"I'm sorry that was so hard on you."

He grinned at her. "And here I was worried about you. You were a tower of strength and I was a puddle of mush."

"Hardly. But even if you had turned into a puddle of mush, you could be excused. Your mother isn't the easiest person to deal with."

The understatement of the year. "Yeah."

Garrett handed him a glass of scotch and he drank, the amber liquid burning a trail to his gut. Lauren's brother raised his glass. "To Cole and Lauren. May you have much happiness in your marriage."

"Hear, hear," Charlotte said, holding up her teacup. Lauren clinked her teacup against Cole's glass.

"To us," she said.

Cole smiled into her eyes, loving her so much his heart ached with it. "To us."

Chapter Eight

November 29

"What do you think of this one?"

Charlotte held up a sleeveless, light blue chiffon concoction of a dress. Lauren frowned.

"I think you're going to freeze in it. It's lovely, but more suited to a warm summer wedding, not a three-weeks-before-Christmas-rush-job wedding."

It was Charlotte's turn to frown. "Are you sure about this, Lauren? I mean, really sure? If you're not, there's still time to back out."

Lauren had thought about her upcoming marriage to Cole long and hard in the days since he'd asked her to marry him. She'd thought about little else. Despite the hurried arrangements, despite his mother's objections, despite keeping secret the fact that Cole was the baby's father, it felt right. It felt absolutely, perfectly *right* to marry Cole.

"I don't want to back out. I want to marry Cole."

Charlotte nodded. "That's good. I'm glad you're sure. I always thought…"

She broke off, shaking her head. Lauren raised an eyebrow.

"Don't hold back now, Char. Come on, spit it out. What do you want to say?"

Charlotte shrugged one slim shoulder, looking

apologetic. "I always thought Cole was the brother you should have married in the first place."

Lauren stared at her, not sure how to respond to that. Perhaps her sister was right. She and Billy had had some good times, at least in the beginning, but their marriage had certainly been less than successful.

Billy had swept her off her feet. Her feelings for Cole had been more about friendship. He made her feel safe, protected, calm.

Was that enough to sustain a marriage?

Taking a deep breath to get herself together, she searched another rack in earnest. A moment later she came up with an emerald green, form-fitting dress with long sleeves. Made of a jersey fabric that promised to hug every curve a woman possessed, it had a modest, cowl neckline, but a deep, plunging, V-shaped back. Lauren pulled it from the rack and handed it to her sister.

"What do you think of this one? It's season appropriate and sexy, in an understated kind of way."

Charlotte held the dress by the hanger and examined it. "You think so? It looks kind of skimpy on the hanger."

"Humor me. Try it on."

She shrugged and headed to the fitting room. Lauren went back to the racks to search for her own dress. It wasn't easy to predict exactly how big she'd be by the time the wedding took place two weeks from now. She had to make sure any dress she chose had room for expansion. Not exactly a requirement of most wedding dresses.

She'd been pregnant at her last wedding, too. It had been the whole reason she and Billy had married. After she'd lost the baby soon after the hastily arranged nuptials, Billy had directed his frustration at her, blaming her for trapping him in a marriage he didn't want. Yet he'd never once asked her for a divorce, giving her hope he wanted to make the marriage work. It had taken her five years to figure out why he'd stayed married to her.

She was starting her marriage to Cole pregnant. Would he grow to resent her the way Billy had?

No. Things would be different this time, she could feel it. Cole was nothing like his brother.

For one thing, he was helping with the arrangements for the wedding. The wedding would be a simple affair at Cole's house, with family and a few close friends in attendance. She'd arranged for a simple meal to be served after the ceremony by her friends from the Homestead Restaurant. The whole thing would be over in an hour or two. Her wedding would be a far cry from the elaborate wedding she'd once dreamed of, with flowers and a wedding cake, and lovely decorations. She pushed those childhood dreams aside, knowing they were unrealistic under the circumstances.

Once the food was in place and they'd secured a judge to perform the ceremony, Cole had said he'd get his house cleaned and readied for the wedding, leaving her little more to do aside from finding a dress and buying him a wedding band. As soon as she and Charlotte had arrived in Fargo for this shopping excursion, they'd gone to a jewelry store and picked out a gold band for Cole. It was understated, yet solid, simple but with some complex and beautiful engraving. To her, the wedding band perfectly expressed Cole's personality.

Charlotte emerged from the fitting room, looking self-conscious as she smoothed a hand over the emerald fabric. "What do you think?"

Lauren couldn't speak for a moment. She was used to her sister in jeans and T-shirts, or in her baggy nurse's scrubs. To see her in the body-hugging dress was a revelation. The dress accentuated her slim build and slender curves. The hem ended a couple of inches above her knees, making her legs appear miles long. The plunging back was tasteful, yet a little daring. The whole effect was sexy. With a capital S.

"Holy crap." Lauren walked around her sister to get the view from all angles. "Holy crap!"

Charlotte made an unhappy face. "Is that a good holy crap or a bad holy crap?"

"Definitely good. Char, you look absolutely stunning!"

"Really?"

Lauren wanted to shake her sister. Or cry for her. Charlotte didn't think of herself as attractive, and hadn't for some time. Lauren remembered the string of boyfriends Charlotte had as a teenager, remembered her outgoing nature and easy confidence, but somewhere along the way, things had changed. If she'd had a serious relationship in the last several years, she hadn't spoken to Lauren about it. Worse, she'd lost confidence in herself as a woman. Her wonderful, smart, accomplished sister deserved to feel like a beautiful, sexy siren.

"Yeah, really! You're gorgeous. No question about it, this is the dress. Wrap it up."

"You don't think it's too revealing?"

"Revealing? No, of course not. Char, you're

covered from your neck to your wrists."

"Yeah, but it's tight." She pulled at the fabric, trying to make it cover her knees. "And short."

"It's not tight, Char. It fits your body perfectly. You probably can't tell because everything you wear is baggy and two sizes too big. And it's not short either. With legs like yours, you should wear dresses like this all the time."

"Really?"

"Yes! Really!" Lauren didn't know what else to say to convince her.

"I thought I looked okay in the dressing room mirror, but I wasn't sure," she said with a frown.

"Well, *I'm* sure. You're beautiful, Char. All you need is a pair of sexy heels and you're set."

Charlotte strained to look at her back in the three-way mirror. "I guess if you think I look all right…maybe with some nice shoes. As long as they don't make me too tall."

Lauren stifled the urge to strangle her sister but was relieved she'd take the dress. "We'll find a shoe store as soon we get out of here. If I ever find a dress, that is."

"Speaking of, I found one hanging in the changing room that might work for you."

Charlotte headed to the back of the store and returned a moment later with a dress. It was a knee-length ivory lace with a scooped neckline and long, unlined lace sleeves that came to a point at the wrist. Best of all, it had an empire waist that promised to camouflage her expanding waistline. An emerald green ribbon beneath the bust line was the only embellishment.

It was perfect. She held her breath as she checked the price tag. To her surprise and relief, the dress was on sale and within her budget. Lauren pumped her fist in the air. Maybe the wedding gods were smiling on her today.

"I think it's a sign," Charlotte said as she touched the ribbon. "We're both meant to wear green on your wedding day. Go try it on and see if it fits."

A few moments later Lauren emerged from the changing room wearing the dress. It fit perfectly, the low cut neckline accentuating her breasts, which with her pregnancy had unexpectedly become her best feature.

As she looked in the mirror, she saw herself as a bride, the first time she'd ever had that sensation. She could imagine standing next to Cole in this dress, reciting her vows.

Charlotte smiled at their reflections in the mirror, her hands resting on Lauren's shoulders.

"Have you found your dress?"

A tear slipped down her cheek, but she was too happy to care.

"Yes, I've found my wedding dress."

****

Two weeks later, on the second weekend in December, Lauren's wedding day dawned cold and clear. She pushed aside the curtains to look out the window of her childhood bedroom. New snow blanketed the front yard of her parents' acreage, making the world clean and bright and fresh. She and Charlotte had stayed overnight with their parents. They'd get ready here and later drive with them the short distance into town to Cole's house.

Her wedding day.

Happiness bubbled in Lauren's heart. Considering the circumstances of her marriage, she should be apprehensive. Instead, she was filled, mind and soul, with the rightness of what she was doing.

Maybe that was because she trusted Cole. She'd never been able to say that about Billy.

She and Charlotte and their mother Grace spent the day getting ready, like a trio of schoolgirls primping for senior prom. As they curled, mascaraed and polished, they laughed. Lauren's father and brother rolled their eyes at their antics. Love for her family overwhelmed her. How lucky she was to have so many people who loved her.

At four-forty-five, they arrived in Masonville for the ceremony, which was scheduled to begin at Cole's house at five. Cars lined both sides of the street in front of his house.

"Is everyone here for the wedding?" Charlotte asked.

Lauren shook her head, confused. "I don't know. As far as I know, it's supposed to be the five of us and Cole's mother and aunt."

"Cole must have invited a few friends."

"I suppose so. Perhaps he asked some people from the clinic."

Garrett dropped everyone off at the front door before driving off to find a parking space. Thankfully Cole had shoveled the snow from the sidewalks. Her high-heeled sandals were not exactly proper winter footwear.

As arranged earlier, they entered the house through the back door, which led to the kitchen. While their parents joined the other guests in the living room, Lauren and Charlotte waited until their father came for them. Isabelle and Greta from the Homestead Restaurant bustled around the kitchen, putting the finishing touches on the buffet dinner. Several large aluminum containers lined the counters, making Lauren wonder who was going to eat all that food. Greta squealed as soon as she saw her.

"Oh, honey, you look so beautiful! What a lovely bride you make!"

Lauren hugged her. "Thank you."

"And you, Miss Charlotte! Wow! You look like you stepped off the runway!"

Charlotte blushed, looking uncomfortable. Lauren wished she could see how beautiful she was.

"How did the wedding cake turn out? Can I see it?" Lauren asked. She'd ordered a sheet cake of Cole's favorite, carrot cake with cream cheese icing.

"We want to surprise you," Isabelle said with a wink. "We did something a little extra special."

"Oh?" That was a surprise. "Thank you."

"Best of luck to you and Cole." Isabelle kissed her cheek. "Greta, can you help me with these appetizers?"

"Yes, of course. Good luck, Lauren!"

Lauren's father returned to the kitchen carrying two bouquets. He handed the smaller bouquet of white peonies and red roses to Charlotte, and gave Lauren the larger bouquet made of red roses and orchids, white holly berries, and green cedar boughs.

"Oh, these are beautiful!" Charlotte breathed.

"Where did they come from, Dad?" Lauren asked, confused.

"Cole gave them to me to give to you girls."

She'd thought the ceremony would be simple and quick, no fuss, no muss. But Isabelle and Greta were obviously planning dinner for far more people than she'd anticipated, and now she and Charlotte had beautiful bouquets. Cole was making this into a real wedding. It was as if he'd guessed her innermost wishes.

For the first time, nervousness made Lauren's stomach swoop. She desperately wanted to be a good wife to him. More than anything she wanted to make him happy. But they were starting their marriage with a lie that made her wonder if she deserved him.

Her father spoke. "Charlotte honey, you go first. Head toward Cole and Garrett. They're standing in front of the fireplace. Lauren and I will follow in a minute."

Charlotte squeezed Lauren's arm before walking out of the kitchen. Her father grasped her hand. She clung tightly to him.

"Are you ready?"

She focused her concentration on breathing in and out, willing her sudden nerves to relax. There was no need to be nervous, she told herself. The people gathered were her friends and family and they only wanted the best for them. And she was marrying Cole, her best friend. The thought calmed her. She smiled at her father.

"Yes. I'm ready."

The first thing Lauren saw as she entered the living room on her father's arm were the flowers. The room was filled with red and white and pink poinsettias. The strains of the wedding march played in the background. The room was filled with people. She saw Audrey and

Evelyn, Dr. Waverly and his wife, and Jamie Garven from the clinic. Ella and her sister were there, as were several neighbors, friends, and relatives.

Then she saw Cole standing next to the fireplace, and she didn't see anyone else. He was her beacon, her lighthouse, and she made her way toward him like a ship to safe harbor.

Finally, she reached him. Her father tenderly kissed her cheek before handing her to Cole and stepping back to stand with her mother. Cole clasped her hands in his, and she drew strength from him. Why had she never before realized how handsome he was? His dark hair gleamed with vitality and his brown eyes smiled warmly into hers. His dark gray suit fit his tall frame perfectly, showing off his broad shoulders and narrow hips.

The judge recited the words of the marriage ceremony, and Lauren responded, staring into Cole's eyes. He looked so happy. She silently vowed to do everything in her power to make sure he stayed that way.

Charlotte handed Cole's ring to her, and she slipped it on his third finger, left hand.

"With this ring, I thee wed."

Cole turned to Garrett, and he passed him her ring. Lauren's hands shook a little as he placed it on her finger. She'd expected something simple, but this wedding band, yellow gold encircled by diamonds, was exquisite. Her breath caught in her throat. She looked up into Cole's face, but he only smiled, his expression calm.

"With this ring, I thee wed," he said.

The gold band sparkled on her hand, a symbol of

his commitment.

Of his love?

Lauren brushed the thought aside. She was getting carried away by the romance of the ceremony. Their marriage was based on friendship and mutual respect. Love didn't enter into the equation.

"I now pronounce you husband and wife. You may kiss the bride."

Cole leaned forward and kissed her. His lips were warm and soft, his kiss tender. She was instantly transported to the last time Cole had kissed her, the night their child was conceived. Memories of warm, wet kisses blew through her head with the power of a hurricane. He'd caressed her, touched her, loved her with a passion and fervor that woke her in the middle of the night wanting more.

Too soon he pulled away. He leaned forward again to whisper in her ear.

"You look beautiful."

"So do you," she whispered back.

The judge addressed the audience. "Ladies and gentlemen, may I present Mr. and Mrs. Cole Walsh."

The crowd cheered and clapped. Garrett whistled. Charlotte came forward to hug and kiss them.

"I'm so happy for both of you," she said, her eyes shiny with tears.

Lauren's parents wished them well, her mother dabbing tears from her eyes. She hugged her and whispered in her ear.

"It'll work this time."

Lauren nodded. *Dear God, I hope she's right.* She couldn't bear another unhappy marriage, especially since this time there'd be a child involved, a child who needed a stable, happy family to grow up in.

But standing beside Cole, with his arm around her shoulders, hope filled her heart.

Ella Walsh got to her feet and made her way toward them. Cole's arm tensed on her shoulders as his mother approached. Lauren set her hand on his back, trying to lend her support.

"Congratulations, Cole, Lauren." Her voice was flat and her face unsmiling. "I wish you a long and happy marriage in which to raise your brother's child."

Cole's jaw clenched, and his fingers dug into her shoulder. After a moment his fingers loosened their grip and he managed a tight smile for his mother.

"Thank you."

Grace came up to Ella and placed her hand on her arm. "Ella, can you help me in the kitchen? Isabelle had some questions about the buffet."

Lauren dipped her head in silent thanks to her mother as she led Ella away. She heard Cole's ragged intake of breath.

"You okay?" she whispered.

"Yeah." With a shake of his head, he turned his attention back to her. "I shouldn't let her get to me, but I do."

"I'm sorry this is so difficult for you."

He squeezed her shoulder again. "No, it's not. Really. I'm happy, Lauren. Very happy."

His words loosened the knot that had formed in her stomach at his mother's words. She smiled in relief.

"I'm glad."

Garrett approached them once more, a short, balding man holding a camera a couple of paces behind him.

"The photographer is hoping to get a few pictures of the happy couple."

Lauren turned to Cole. "We have a photographer?"

"Sure. Isn't that what people do at weddings? Take pictures?"

It was, but Lauren hadn't expected photos to be taken at her wedding. The only pictures she had of her wedding to Billy were a few shots Charlotte had snapped with her phone.

They posed for the camera, sometimes alone and sometimes with their parents or their bridal party. Fortunately, the photographer kept up a steady banter that kept them all smiling and relaxed.

"How about the bride and groom alone, but this time, Mr. Groom, I want to see you give your brand-new wife a big fat kiss. I know you've got it in you."

Everyone laughed, including Cole. A blush heated Lauren's cheeks and she guessed they were likely as red as a sunburn. *Won't that be lovely in the wedding album?*

Cole kissed her and she forgot to be self-conscious, forgot her own name. His sweet, lingering kiss hinted at the passion bubbling inside him. But there was also tenderness and affection, and something she couldn't name, some deep, driving emotion. She cupped his face with her hand, needing to touch him.

Too soon he broke the kiss. He stared into her eyes, and her heart leapt at the desire she saw there.

"Thank you very much," the photographer said. He pressed a business card into Cole's hand. "I'll be in touch with you in a few days, and we can set up a time for you to look at the photos and pick out the ones you want to keep."

Cole fumbled with the card as if having trouble concentrating on what the man was saying.

"Yes, that will be fine. Thanks for coming."

The photographer nodded and headed off. Soon Isabelle and Greta began circling the room with trays of appetizers while Garrett and Tom Waverly manned a makeshift bar set up in one corner of the room. A steady stream of well-wishers offered their congratulations.

For the first time Lauren noticed the tiny, sparkling lights that had been strung around the room. They gave the room a festive, celebratory air.

Like a real wedding.

Lauren raised her bouquet to her face and caught the sweet scent of the red roses. She hadn't expected flowers or lights or cameras. She hadn't even expected guests beyond family. The fact that Cole had gone to so much trouble both stunned and delighted her. It told her how invested he was in this marriage.

The cynic in her argued that he wanted the marriage to work because of the baby. But her optimistic side countered there was more than practicality in his kiss. There'd been…something. Something wild and elemental.

Something she wanted to explore.

A beautiful buffet dinner was served soon after. Guests filled their plates in the kitchen and brought them into the living room, where they ate with their plates on their laps. Garrett and a couple of cousins set up a folding table in front of the fireplace for the bridal party and their parents. After everyone finished eating, Garrett rose to make a toast, a glass in his hand.

"I'd like to welcome Cole into our family. He's a

good friend and a good man, and I wish him every happiness." He lifted his glass. "Ladies and gentlemen, to the groom."

"To the groom."

Glasses clinked together around the room. Lauren sipped sparkling grape juice from the champagne glass Garrett handed her.

"And to my beautiful sister Lauren," Garrett continued. He paused, his voice choking up. "May you have everything you've always wanted. Everything you deserve. May your skies always be clear and blue. And may your life be filled with health and love and happiness." He raised his glass once more. "To the bride."

"To the bride."

Lauren held out a hand to Garrett, and he caught it, bringing it to his lips for a kiss. Tears prickled at the back of her eyes. She loved her brother so much. They'd almost lost him in Afghanistan. But he was home now and safe, though she sometimes saw a bleakness in his eyes that he tried to hide.

She loved her family. Their support had been the only thing that had made her marriage to Billy, and his death, bearable.

Cole got to his feet. "Thank you for your kind words and your warm welcome, Garrett. I want to thank everyone for coming, and for making this day so special for Lauren and me. And now I think Isabelle and Greta have a surprise for us."

Lauren wasn't sure she could take many more surprises. But she was delighted to see Isabelle and Greta push a trolley into the room containing a large three-layered cake decorated with red roses made of spun sugar.

"It's fancier than I imagined it would be, but I love it. It's beautiful," Lauren whispered.

"I had a word with Isabelle. I thought we should have something memorable."

Lauren glanced at the cake once more, and turned back to him with a smile. "It's lovely. I'll always remember it. Thank you."

His brown eyes were warm and happy. "My pleasure."

"I hope the cake is still the flavor I asked for. I wanted carrot cake with cream cheese icing. I hope it's still your favorite," she said.

"It *is* my favorite," he said in surprise. "How did you know?"

"I remembered." She'd made one back in high school that he'd raved about. She'd never forgotten.

"Come on, tell the truth. You asked my mother, didn't you?"

"Maybe. Or maybe not."

Cole laughed and shook his head. He stood and held out his hand to her. "Come on. Let's cut the cake. I want a piece."

They cut the cake together, posing for photos. Lauren couldn't remember ever smiling so much in pure happiness.

Once the guests finished dessert and coffee, they began to file out of the house, extending their well wishes to Lauren and Cole as they left. Ella caught a ride home with her sister, saying a perfunctory goodbye to her and simply nodding at Cole. Lauren wished she'd recognize how hurtful her indifference was to him.

Isabelle and Greta tidied the kitchen and packed up

their equipment. Greta gave Lauren a warm hug.

"I'm so happy for you, sweetie," she said. "I'm glad something good could come of the tragedy you experienced." She leaned in closer, whispering in her ear. "Between you and me, your husband is one fine-looking man. And a good one, too. Not many men would be happy about raising another man's child, even if it is his brother's. But Cole, he's one in a million."

Lauren swallowed. Is that what people thought, that Cole was some kind of saint for taking her in and accepting her child? She supposed that was better than believing the two of them had been having an affair all through her marriage. She sighed. Some people probably believed that, too. In a small town like Masonville, people lived in each other's pockets, and she couldn't control what they believed, or gossiped about.

Soon only a few friends and family remained. Garrett and the cousins began stacking chairs and taking them away. Her mother and sister collected garbage and swept the hardwood floors, while Cole and her father took down the lights and moved the living room furniture back into place. The house was soon back to normal.

Audrey returned with Brady from the clinic where he'd spent the day. The dog strained at his leash, eager to get to Cole. They greeted each other as if they'd been apart for months instead of only a day. Lauren laughed at their roughhousing.

"Thanks for getting him for me, Audrey. I owe you one," Cole said, fending off Brady's eager kisses.

"No problem." She embraced Lauren. "It was a lovely wedding. Thank you for inviting me."

"Thank you so much for coming and for looking after Brady. I'll see you on Monday at work."

"You're coming to work on Monday? Aren't you going away for a little honeymoon?"

Honeymoon? The thought hadn't crossed her mind. But Cole had surprised her with so many things today, she couldn't be sure.

He put his arm around her shoulders. "Maybe once the baby arrives we'll go on a little trip, but for now, we'll stay close to home."

She squeezed his hand in silent thanks. Even though the pregnancy was going well now, he understood she would be uneasy about travelling and being far away from her family and her doctor. They hadn't spoken about it, but somehow he'd known, the same way he'd known the bouquets, and decorations, and the guests meant so much to her.

How did he know her so well?

Garrett left to take the chairs back to the community center. Audrey left, and a couple of moments later her parents and Charlotte said their goodbyes as well, embracing both of them on their way out.

Aside from Brady, they were alone. Nerves skittered down her spine.

"Tired?" Cole asked.

She stifled a yawn. "I'm fine."

"Liar," he said with a grin. "Come sit down and put your feet up. Would you like some tea or maybe hot chocolate?"

"You have hot chocolate?"

"Don't get too excited. It's only the instant, powdered kind."

"Works for me. If you have mini marshmallows, you'll have truly made my night."

"Sorry, no marshmallows of any size."

She sighed dramatically. "Oh, well. I'll excuse it this time, but from now on we really need to keep mini marshmallows in the house for all my hot chocolate emergencies."

He chuckled as he led her to the sofa and lifted her feet onto the ottoman. "I'll put it on the grocery list."

He went to the kitchen to make the hot chocolate, while Brady curled into a ball next to the sofa. Lauren leaned back against the sofa cushions with a contented sigh and surveyed the room. The poinsettias still ringed the living room, lending a festive atmosphere. It had been such a wonderful day, and such a beautiful ceremony. Cole had gone to so much trouble…

She lifted her left hand and examined her wedding ring. The circle of diamonds sparkled in the dim evening light. The ring was so beautiful, so *special.* Cole had obviously taken a great deal of care in choosing it. She couldn't have picked a more perfect ring. It was exactly the kind of ring she'd always dreamed of.

Lauren glanced around the living room once more, her gaze skimming over the red brick fireplace, the scratched wooden floor peeking out from around the worn red-and-blue area rug, the bold orange-and-yellow-flowered wallpaper covering the dining room walls that had to be a remnant of the seventies. She smiled fondly. Despite the questionable decorating, the house surrounded her with happiness. It was more than bricks and mortar. It was a home.

Her home. From now on this house was where she

would live. With Cole. And their child.

The realization made her breath hitch. Her next thought robbed her of breath.

This is my wedding night.

Images rushed through her mind as she closed her eyes. Cole undressing her, touching her with gentle hands, caressing her. The look in his eyes, so fierce, yet so loving—

"Here you go. One cup of instant hot chocolate, minus the mini marshmallows."

Lauren sat up with a start, blinking open her eyes. Cole stood over her, a steaming mug in his hand. He frowned, two vertical lines forming between his brows.

"I'm sorry. I didn't mean to startle you. Did you fall asleep?"

"No, I'm fine. I mean, I wasn't asleep." Her blush heated her face. There was no way she could tell him what she'd been daydreaming about. "I was resting my eyes, that's all."

He handed her the mug and sat next to her. His eyes filled with concern as he tucked a wayward curl behind her ear.

"You're tired. It's been a long day. You should get some rest."

"I'm fine, really." She attempted a smile. "Especially now that I have chocolate."

A grin quirked his lips before being replaced by the look of concern once more. "Drink your chocolate and then go to bed."

Lauren averted her gaze and sipped the hot liquid. "Aren't you coming to bed too?"

Silence greeted her question, and she was too afraid to look into his face. Had she only imagined passion in his kiss? Maybe she'd fooled herself into believing Cole's feelings for her extended beyond obligation.

Finally, she heard his sigh. "You should get some sleep. I'll sleep in the spare room."

"Cole—"

"Your suitcases are in the master bedroom. Garrett brought them over this afternoon. I've made room for your things in the closet."

Disappointment swamped her. *He doesn't want me.* She still couldn't look at him. "Thank you."

"There's a new mattress on the bed. It's very comfortable."

Then why won't you share it with me? She squeezed her eyes shut. "That's good. Thanks."

"Lauren? Are you okay?"

She forced herself to open her eyes and turn to him with a smile. If he didn't want to sleep with her, she wouldn't make him feel guilty about it.

"I guess you're right. I am a little tired."

He squeezed her shoulder gently. "You can sleep as late as you like tomorrow. No one's going to bother you."

For God's sake, bother me! She wanted to scream at him, shake him. Instead she nodded. "Okay."

She drained her mug as quickly as she could, the enjoyment she usually derived from chocolate eluding her. Setting her mug on a side table, she lifted her legs from the ottoman and slid to the edge of the sofa. Cole was on his feet in a second, putting a hand under her elbow to help her stand. Brady jumped up as well, his tail wagging.

"I'll see you in the morning," she said. "Good

night."

Cole dropped his hand, leaving Lauren cold and bereft. "Good night. Sleep well."

Brady followed her into the master bedroom and jumped onto the bed, circling a few times before lying down and making himself comfortable. Lauren sighed. At least one male in this family wanted to sleep with her.

Chapter Nine

December 13

Her skin flowed through his hands like warm silk. So soft. So fragrant. So utterly enticing. His hands trembled as he touched her, and he reminded himself to go slow, to prolong her pleasure as long as he could. He wanted to please her, needed to please her.

Anything to make her stay.

Lauren's breath caught. She arched her back and made tiny noises in her throat that told him she liked when he touched her breasts, when he rubbed her nipple between his thumb and forefinger. He took the nipple in his mouth, loving the inarticulate sounds of pleasure she made as he teased and licked and worshipped her body. She tasted sweet, and intoxicating, like the finest wine. Her small hands tangled in his hair.

"Please Cole, please," she begged.

His control hung by a thread. He struggled to hang on. Nudging her thighs open, he pushed against the opening to her body. Tremors raced through her body as her hands moved restlessly over his back and buttocks.

"I need you. Please, please, please."

He slid inside her, her heat surrounding him. A feeling of homecoming enveloped him. This was where he belonged. With the woman he loved. The woman he'd always loved.

Slowly, he withdrew. Then he thrust into her, hard and fast. He withdrew again, thrust again, over and over and over. The pleasure was so intense he thought he would fly into a million pieces. He could feel his orgasm rising, wanting to break free, but he pushed it back. He needed her to fly first.

Her arms tightened around him and her body bowed as her release came. She cried out.

"Cole! I love you!"

Cole nearly cried at hearing her say those words. He'd loved Lauren forever, longed for her, and now she was finally his. He held her, teetering on the edge of release, knowing his climax would take him someplace he'd never been before. Almost there—

Cole awoke abruptly, his body drenched in sweat and on the verge of release. Pushing himself to a sitting position, he breathed in deep, ragged breaths until his body was once more under control.

He groaned. He hadn't had a wet dream since he was fourteen. But he'd never had a desirable woman sleeping down the hall before either. An untouchably desirable woman.

He groaned again and slid out of bed. After putting on jeans and a T-shirt, he padded barefoot out of the room. Checking down the hall, he saw that the door to the master bedroom was closed. He hoped Lauren was sleeping better than he was.

Quietly, he made his way to the kitchen and flicked on the light switch. Before his eyes adjusted to the light, he heard a shriek and the sound of glass breaking.

"Cole! Geez, you scared the life out of me! You made me drop my glass."

He rubbed his eyes. “Lauren? What are you doing up? Are you okay?”

“Yes, I’m fine. I couldn’t sleep.” She raised her hand in a stopping motion as he stepped toward her. “Stay where you are until I clean up this mess.”

She tiptoed gingerly around the shards, and after retrieving a broom and dust pan from the closet, she swept up the broken glass.

“Is there something wrong with the furnace?” She dropped the pieces into the garbage can. “It’s freezing in here.”

“The furnace is fine. I always sleep at this temperature.”

“Really? I was so cold I couldn’t sleep. And Brady hogged all the blankets. I thought maybe some warm milk would help. I’m sorry, did I wake you?”

“No, I couldn’t sleep either.”

She shivered. “I guess I’m going to have to invest in thermal pajamas. And maybe an extra duvet.”

For the first time he noticed she had a blanket slung around her shoulders, over her robe. “You really are cold, aren’t you?”

“I’m freezing.”

He grabbed her hand. “Come on. We need to warm you up.”

Leading her into the living room, he made her sit on the sofa. He tucked the blanket securely around her before using the remote control to turn on the gas fireplace. It began throwing out heat in seconds.

Lauren covered a yawn with her hand. “I didn’t know this was a gas fireplace.”

“It used to be wood burning, but after Grandpa died, Grandma had it converted to gas. She didn’t want to haul wood and ashes anymore."

A volley of sharp barks came from the bedroom. Lauren groaned and threw off the blanket. "I left Brady in the bedroom. I guess he woke up."

Cole gently pushed her back against the sofa cushions and pulled up the blanket once more. "I'll take care of Brady. You stay here and get warm."

Before she could put up an argument, he left the room. Brady bounded from the bedroom as soon as he opened the door. Cole found him curled next to Lauren on the sofa as he returned to the living room with a mug of warm milk for her.

"Brady, down. You know you're not allowed on the sofa."

The dog gave him a doleful glance before jumping down and lying on the floor between the sofa and the coffee table, as close to Lauren as possible. Cole handed her the mug.

"So much for man's best friend. One look at you and he threw me over without a second thought." Not that he blamed the dog.

Lauren bent to scratch Brady's ears. "Don't worry. You're still his best bud. I've got the newness factor working for me at the moment. Isn't that right, Brady?"

The dog looked up at her with adoring eyes before lovingly licking her hand. Cole chuckled as he sat next to her. "Oh, yeah. I can see he's only pretending to be crazy about you."

She leaned back against the sofa and sipped her hot milk. "It's a total act. He'll soon figure out where his kibble is coming from."

God, she was beautiful. Even in a worn terrycloth robe, with her long hair mussed from sleep, she was the most beautiful woman he'd ever known. He wanted to tell her the thoughts in his heart, wanted to declare his love. The words trembled on his tongue. Most of all, he wanted to gather her in his arms and take her to his bed, to sink so deep inside her that he forgot where he ended and she began.

But he was afraid she didn't feel the same way. Someday, he hoped, she'd come to love him. But for now he had to take things slow.

"How's the milk?" he asked, searching for something to say.

"Kind of disgusting, actually. But it usually helps me sleep." Her eyes were already at half-mast.

"Are you feeling warmer?"

She yawned. "Yeah. Except my feet."

Her bare feet were propped on the coffee table, looking impossibly pretty with their pink toenails. Cole leaned forward and lifted her right foot, gently rubbing to lend it some of his warmth. Then he did the same with the left foot.

"Is that better?"

She smiled sleepily. "Mmm. Yes, thank you."

"I'll get you another blanket."

She laid her hand on his arm. "No, don't go. Stay with me for a while. Please?"

"Sure, okay." There was nowhere else he'd rather be.

He sat back, and Lauren snuggled against him, bringing up her knees and tucking her feet beneath the blanket. She rested her head on his shoulder, her left hand on his chest, against his heart. He noticed she hadn't taken off her wedding ring, but then neither had he. He wrapped his arm around her, his heart so full of love for her he was afraid it might burst out of his chest.

"I love my ring, Cole." She lifted her head to look into his eyes. "I couldn't imagine anything more beautiful. The wedding was wonderful. Everything was so lovely—the flowers, the cake, the bouquets. Thank you. You made me feel like a real bride."

"You are a real bride."

Her eyes clouded at that, frown lines appearing on her brow as if she didn't believe him. She averted her gaze, settling against his side once more. Cole hugged her even closer.

"You looked beautiful today. I've never seen a more beautiful bride."

"You think so?"

"Yes, of course I do. You looked happy, too. Were you happy today, Lauren?"

She relaxed against him on a sigh. "Yes, very happy."

He kissed her hair, his lips lingering against the fragrant strands. "That's good. I want you to be happy." *With me.*

"You, too." She was nearly asleep. "You'll stay?"

"I'm right here, sweetheart."

Forever.

****

Lauren woke slowly, trying to get her bearings. Though the curtains were still drawn, she could tell from the light seeping in around their edges that it had to be mid-morning. She was in the master bedroom once more, warm and comfortable in the large bed. An extra duvet had been thrown over her. Cole must have carried her here sometime during the night and covered her with an extra blanket to keep her warm.

Cole. She smiled to herself, tenderness swamping her. He took such good care of her. She'd never been treated like something precious before, but she could get used to it.

A warm weight snuggled against her side. Lauren grinned. She hadn't pegged Cole to be such a cuddler.

Pulling an arm out from beneath the blankets, she reached out to touch him. Her hand was met by the feel of a wet nose, warm fur and an affectionate lick. She pulled herself to a sitting position.

"Brady! What are you doing here again? Where's Cole?"

The dog responded by rolling onto his back in anticipation of a tummy rub. To Brady's delight, Lauren complied with some desultory scratches. His tongue lolled out the side of his mouth.

"I love you, too, Buddy, but I'd rather wake up with your master."

Disappointment brought tears to her eyes. She stopped scratching to put her hand over her mouth to stop her sob. The last thing she wanted was for Cole to hear her crying. Had he stayed with her in this bed for a while, or had he dropped her off and made his escape to the spare room?

She glanced at the other side of the bed. The blankets hadn't been turned down and the pillows were unused. Only the top of the blankets, where Brady had slept, had been disturbed.

She had her answer. Did Cole ever intend to sleep with her?

Brady whined and snuggled close, picking up on her distress. She hugged him around his neck, taking comfort in his big, furry presence. Finally, she sucked in a breath and wiped away her tears with the back of her hand.

"Enough with the tears, right, boy? Time to get out of bed."

She slid her feet to the cold floor and found her robe on a nearby chair. Cole must have taken off her robe after he brought her to the bedroom. He'd been so sweet last night. He'd held her so tenderly. For a short time, she'd felt cherished. But she woke alone. Aside from Brady, of course.

Lauren sighed. She'd told herself she couldn't make him have feelings he didn't have. But it was so confusing. Sometimes, like last night as he'd held her in his arms, they were in complete harmony. But this morning he was gone.

He'd said he wanted a real marriage, including sex. So why wouldn't he touch her?

Frustrated, she headed to the bathroom and had a long, hot shower. The streaming water helped to put her feelings into perspective. She and Cole had found themselves in an exceedingly awkward situation. She had to be patient, to take it slow. They'd been friends for a long time. They'd get over this awkward stage to be friends again. And maybe their friendship would grow into something more.

Why was it so important for her to have that "something more" with Cole? She was honest enough with herself to realize she wanted him. But was it true attraction or simply a byproduct of her crazy pregnancy hormones? Were these feelings only for him?

Her questions were answered the moment she walked into the kitchen. Cole looked up from the eggs he was scrambling and smiled at her, and Lauren knew she didn't want anyone else in the world.

"Good morning," he said.

"Good morning." She glanced at the clock on the stove and was shocked to discover it was almost noon. "More like good afternoon. I didn't realize it was so late. You should have woken me."

"No way. Did you sleep well?"

"I slept very well, thank you." It was on the tip of her tongue to add she wished she hadn't slept alone, but she bit back the comment. "Smells good in here. Are you baking something?"

"Blueberry muffins. They'll be out of the oven in about five minutes."

"I'm impressed. I didn't know you baked."

He chuckled and reached for a package on the counter. "I don't. But I managed to add eggs and water to the muffin mix. I think we should be safe."

"I'm still impressed." That he'd go to so much trouble for her warmed her heart. She grinned at the flowered apron tied around his waist. "Nice apron. Very…pink."

His cheeks turned as pink as the apron at her teasing. "It was my grandma's. It was the only one I could find."

"I liked your Grandma Morris. She was a real no-nonsense kind of person. You always knew where you stood with her."

"She liked you, too."

That was a surprise. "Really? I always thought she was kind of disappointed that Billy married me."

Cole kept his eyes on the eggs he was beating. "It wasn't you. She thought Billy was too immature to marry so young."

"Oh." Grandma Morris had certainly been right about that. In hindsight, Lauren recognized she'd probably been too young and immature as well.

"I miss her."

Lauren heard the sadness in his voice. His mother's unhealthy attachment to Billy meant Cole and Ella had never been close. He'd turned to his grandparents, especially his grandmother, for love and attention. But now his grandparents and his father were gone, and Ella was lost in mourning Billy. Cole was alone.

No, he wasn't. She and the baby were Cole's family now. It would take some time to get used to thinking of herself as his wife rather than simply his friend.

"Would you like some coffee?"

She shook her head. "No, thanks."

She used to have a small caffeine addiction, but since she'd been pregnant she hadn't been able to tolerate the stuff. Even the smell still bothered her a little, but at least it didn't nauseate her anymore.

"How about hot chocolate or tea?"

"Do you have green tea?"

He rummaged in a cupboard and pulled out a small box. "You're in luck. I'll put on the kettle. Are you hungry?"

"Starved. I could eat a side of beef."

He grinned at her. "Maybe we've got a little linebacker in there."

"Maybe. Now that the morning sickness is over, I've got this voracious appetite. I'm afraid I'm going to turn into a blimp."

"If you do, you'll be the prettiest blimp in Masonville."

"That's not funny, Cole." But she couldn't help but laugh.

He intertwined her fingers with his, his expression growing serious. "You're going to be one of those mothers-to-be who glow. You're going to be as beautiful in the last stage of your pregnancy as you are now."

He kissed her hand, his gaze never leaving her face. His dark eyes were filled with tenderness. Sudden panic gripped her. She was having Cole's baby. She was responsible for their happiness. What if she messed up? What if she was a lousy mother? A lousy wife? She hadn't exactly done a stellar job the first time.

Without warning, tears welled up behind her eyes, and a hiccupping sob burst from her mouth. She put her free hand over her mouth to stop the tears, but they came anyway.

"Hey, what's this?" He pulled her into his arms and held her tightly.

"I'm sorry," she said against his chest. She clutched the soft denim of his shirt, needing his support, needing to touch him, to be held by him. "Everything makes me cry these days. I can't seem to stop. The other day I found myself crying over a cell phone commercial on TV."

He kissed the top of her hair and chuckled. "It's okay, sweetheart. It's the hormones running amuck."

"You didn't ask for any of this." She buried her face against his chest, unable to look into his face. "You didn't ask for a crazy, emotional wife, or to get kicked out of your own bed. You didn't ask for a baby who's going to need your emotional and financial support for the next twenty years. I've totally disrupted your life, turned everything upside down. I'm so sorry, Cole."

"Lauren, look at me." He grasped her by the shoulders and held her at arm's length, then tipped up her chin to force her to meet his eyes. "This isn't all on you. I was there when our child was conceived, and as I recall, I was a willing participant. It's not as if you forced me into anything against my will."

"Yes, but—"

Cole stopped her words with a gentle finger over her lips. "Yes, my life's been changed, but it's a good change. The best change. We're going to have a baby, sweetheart. That is such an incredible miracle! I can't even tell you how happy that makes me."

She wiped her eyes with trembling fingers. "Really?"

"Really." The look in his sincere brown eyes told her he meant it. "And I'm lucky to have you as my wife. You're my best friend. I know sometimes this marriage and parenthood thing isn't going to be easy, but we'll figure it out together, okay?"

She touched his stubble-covered face, loving the rough feel of it under her fingers.

"Okay. I'll try to keep the waterworks under control."

He grinned. "Deal."

The timer dinged on the stove, indicating the muffins were ready to come out of the oven. With a final squeeze, Cole dropped his hands from her shoulders.

"I'd better get that. We need to feed our linebacker."

Lauren wiped away a leftover tear. Maybe the pregnancy was keeping him from sleeping with her.

Maybe he was afraid of hurting her or the baby. She wanted to ask, but was too afraid. What if he simply didn't want her? She forced a smile.

"Yes, we do. What else are we having for breakfast?"

"Whatever you want, sweetheart."

Chapter Ten

December 14

"So what do you want to do for the rest of the day?" Cole put the last plate on the drainboard and dried his hands on a towel hanging on the oven door. Lauren sat at the table, her hands wrapped around her mug of green tea as she watched fat flakes of snow tumble to the earth on the other side of the kitchen window. Something about the way the winter light fell across her face made her look so heartbreakingly beautiful that his chest ached.

She turned to him with a smile. "I don't have any big plans. Please don't feel like you have to entertain me. And for the record, I'm pregnant, not sick. I could have helped you with the dishes."

Cole refilled his mug with coffee and brought it to the table. "I know. This is a one-day reprieve from work. Tomorrow it's back to reality."

The truth was he wanted to swathe her in bubble wrap and protect her and the baby for the duration of her pregnancy. He would happily do all the housework and cooking. Even though her job didn't entail any heavy lifting or hours on her feet, he wished she would take it easy for the next four and a half months, her only work the successful completion of her pregnancy and the delivery of a healthy baby.

But he understood Lauren well enough to realize staying home would drive her nuts. She was the kind of person who wanted to do things, to accomplish goals. She was also the kind of person who wanted to pay her own way. Relying on him for financial support would hurt her pride.

She sipped on her tea before smiling at him. "Reality's not so bad, but it is nice to have a day off. Did you have anything in mind you wanted to do?"

"I was thinking about the third bedroom, the one closest to the master bedroom. I think it would make a good nursery. I thought maybe we could look online at paint samples and floor coverings." He crooked his thumb toward the kitchen wall, the one covered with fluorescent pink-and-green-flowered wallpaper. "You might have noticed my grandmother had a penchant for bright colors. Right now, all four walls of that bedroom are covered with the most hideous wallpaper I've ever seen."

"Your grandmother certainly had interesting taste," she said with a grin. "My personal favorite is the dining room wallpaper. It really brightens up the room."

"I hope you're being sarcastic, because that wallpaper is almost uglier than the stuff in the bedroom. This is a great, solid little house, and I'm grateful to Grandma for leaving it to me, but it really needs redecorating." He looked at the wallpaper again and shook his head. "The amount of work it needs is overwhelming. I don't know where to start."

"We'll tackle one job at a time, starting with the nursery. I think it'll be fun to get the room ready for the baby." She bit her lip, her brow creasing in a frown. "Did I tell you your mother has offered to buy a crib?

Actually, she insisted on it. I looked it up online. It's a high-end crib, very beautiful, but very expensive. I feel bad about taking her money."

"There's nothing you can do. Once my mother decides on something, she won't back down." He wondered if she'd be prepared to spend so much money if she knew the baby was his and not his brother's.

"She's already ordered the crib. It's supposed to arrive in the next couple of weeks. You don't think she's overextended herself, do you? I mean, is she going to leave herself short for rent?"

"No, that's not going to happen."

"How can you be sure?"

"Because I'm paying the rent on her apartment."

Lauren blinked at him in surprise. "Oh. I didn't know."

He heaved a sigh. "She gets a small pension from Dad's Social Security. It's not enough to support her, so I stepped in to help her out. The alternative would have been to have her move in with me. I figured paying the rent on her own apartment was the lesser evil."

He didn't mean to sound bitter. After all these years he should be used to his mother's preference of his brother over him. But it still stung.

His mother probably wished he'd died instead of Billy.

Lauren reached across the table and linked her fingers with his. "You're a good son."

He blew out a breath and looked away. "Hardly."

"Yes, you are." She tightened her grip on his hand. "I'm sorry Ella doesn't appreciate everything you do for her. I'm sorry she doesn't realize what a wonderful person you are."

He couldn't speak. He simply stared into her compassionate green eyes and clung to her hand as if she was his lifeline.

Maybe she was.

His cell phone rang, and the moment was over. Regretfully, he released her hand and reached for the phone clipped to his belt. Jamie Garven's number was on the screen.

"Hi, Jamie. What's up?"

"I'm really sorry to bother you the day after your wedding, but we've got a problem," she said apologetically. "Des Murphy's mare is in trouble. She's in labor, her waters have broken, and the foal's front feet have emerged, but not the head. Des thinks the head is bent back at an awkward angle that won't allow the foal to be delivered. Dr. Waverly is doing an emergency caesarian at the Sunshine Dairy Farm, so he's unavailable. I've never delivered a foal. I thought the mare and foal would have a better chance if you were there."

So much for spending the day with my new wife. "You did the right thing. I'll get out there as soon as I can. But in the meantime, call Des and tell him to get his mare up and walking. Sometimes the foal can reposition itself properly if the mare walks around a while. Whatever he does, tell him not to pull on the forelegs. That will only make things worse."

"Okay, I'll call him back right now. I'll give him your instructions and tell him you're on your way. And again, I'm really sorry."

"Don't worry about it. I'll talk to you later."

He disconnected the call and clipped the cell phone back onto his belt as he got to his feet. Lauren rose at the same time.

"I'm sorry, I've got an emergency. Occupational hazard of being a country vet."

"I'll come with you."

"What? No! It's cold out there. I've got a mare with a possible breach birth. It could take hours." *And the outcome might not be good.*

"I want to see you in action," she said. "I can hold stuff for you, get coffee, whatever. I'll be your gopher."

"I don't want you to get a chill. This could take hours. You'll be bored sitting around all day."

"I'll be bored sitting around here all day waiting for you. I'll dress warmly. I'll even take a couple of extra blankets. If I get cold, I'll sit in your truck for a while. And I'll bring a book to pass the time."

"You're sure about this?"

"Absolutely."

He didn't have time to argue. "Okay, this goes against my better judgment, but you can come, providing you're ready to go in five minutes."

She grinned as she ran from the room. "I'll be ready."

She was good as her word. In less than five minutes, she was waiting for him at the front door. Before heading out to the farm, they made a quick stop at the clinic. As Cole loaded medical supplies into the truck, he did a fast inventory in his head and hoped he had everything he'd need to help the mare. With any luck, the foal would reposition itself and deliver naturally. There was no time to get the mare into his antiseptically clean surgery. He didn't like the idea of doing a caesarian section in a barn where the risk of infection was high, but if it meant saving the life of the foal or the mare, or both, he'd do it.

Lauren sat quietly next to him in the truck. "Are you worried?"

"Any time you go into a situation like this, it's a worry. Every mare is different and each birth is different. The vast majority of equine births happen naturally and without problems, but if something goes wrong, it can go spectacularly wrong in a hell of hurry."

"You'll help her," she said confidently.

Cole glanced at her. Her smile told him she had every confidence he'd do the right things for the mare. It was humbling to know she had so much faith in him.

They arrived at Des Murphy's farm in less than twenty minutes from the time he'd received Jamie's call. Cole drove through the yard and past the house, making his way straight to the barn and the paddock beyond. Luckily, he'd been to the farm on numerous occasions and knew his way around.

Des met them at the barn door. Cole shook his hand. "Des, this is my wife, Lauren. Lauren, Des Murphy. He's been a client of mine since I moved back to Masonville." Introducing Lauren as his wife made his chest swell with pride.

"I heard you got married. Yesterday, right, Doc? Congratulations."

"Thanks. Where's your mare, Des?"

"She's here in the barn. I got her up and was walking her around like you said, and the forelegs went back inside. But a couple of minutes ago, she stopped and wouldn't go anymore. She's lying down on her side again."

Hopefully, that meant she was ready to deliver, and with any luck the foal had gotten its act together and was positioned to make a proper entrance into the world. As they reached the stall, Cole saw that the mare was indeed on her side, her rear end facing them. Des opened the latch and quietly walked into the stall. Cole turned to Lauren and spoke in a quiet voice before following him.

"It's best you stay out here. We don't want to spook her with too many people." Horses had the ability to completely stop labor if feeling threatened in any way. Cole wanted to avoid that possibility.

Lauren nodded and stood in a spot outside the stall where she could watch but not be detected by the mare. Cole entered the stall and closed the gate quietly behind him. Des was bent by the mare's head, patting her nose.

"It's all right now, Sophie girl. The vet's here to help you."

Cole slipped off his jacket. Des had already brought a bucket of warm water and a container of antibacterial soap to the stall. Cole carefully washed Sophie's perineum in preparation for his examination.

"Des, can you hold Sophie's tail out of the way for me?"

Des quickly complied, lifting the tail, which he had already wrapped with fabric in preparation for the birth. Cole pulled a clean examination sleeve from his medical kit and slipped it on, then covered it liberally with a water-soluble lubricant.

"I'm going to examine Sophie to see if I can feel the foal and how it's positioned in the birth canal." He spoke in a quiet, low voice so as not to startle the mare. He gently patted her rump with his ungloved hand. "Easy now, Sophie."

Parting the vulva, he inserted his hand and pushed

in nearly all the way to his shoulder.

"There's the nose. The foal's head is facing the right way."

"That's a girl, Sophie. I knew you could do it," Des said.

They weren't out of the woods yet. Cole moved his hand again, wincing as a contraction squeezed his forearm. A second later he touched the hooves of two tiny forelegs.

"We've got two forelegs where they should be. I have to make sure the back legs aren't tucked under the foal's body. We can't deliver the foal naturally unless the back legs are splayed out behind it."

If the legs were tucked underneath its body, he'd have no choice but to perform a C-section. A foal in that position would never make it through the birth canal.

He moved his hand beneath the foal and felt for the other two feet, but could find nothing. He breathed a sigh of relief. Almost there.

"It looks like the foal's in the right position. We're going to give Sophie a little help to have this baby."

Cole attached obstetrical ropes to the forelegs, and after applying lubricant to the canal to ease the baby along the way, he and Des both gently pulled, being careful to exert a slight twisting motion to allow the foal to follow the natural anatomy of the birth canal. They pulled one leg a little more than the other so that it would be delivered first, followed by the other leg, and finally by the head, as if it was a totally natural birth. If the traction didn't work and the foal wasn't born quickly, he might still have to perform an emergency C-section.

Sophie lifted her head and whinnied. A contraction slowed their progress, pulling the foal back a bit. But despite that, one tiny foreleg soon emerged from the vulva.

"Good girl, Sophie. Just a little more."

They continued to pull, and a minute later the other foreleg appeared. A moment after that the nose was visible. Sophie seemed to sense the end was near. She pushed, her body rocking as if she was getting to her feet. The foal slid out onto the straw, the amniotic sac tearing open and the umbilical cord breaking as the foal was expelled from its mother, exactly as it was supposed to.

"You did it, Sophie girl. You did it!" Des gently stroked the mare's flanks. Sophie pushed herself to her feet and sniffed at her new baby, gently licking its nose and nudging it as if encouraging it to try out its new, spindly legs. Kneeling next to the foal, Cole placed his stethoscope on its chest to take its heart rate, and was pleased by the strong, steady hundred beats per minute. Its eyes were bright and open and its tongue and lips were a normal light pink, indicating it was breathing normally. Once he'd satisfied himself that all was well, he stepped to the side, not wanting to get in the way of the developing bond between mother and baby.

"Cole, that was so beautiful!" Lauren whispered. She stood behind the stall's gate, her hands wrapped around the iron bars and tears shining in her beautiful green eyes. "Is it a boy or a girl?"

He wanted to touch her but hadn't had a chance to wash up. Grinning at her, he said, "I can't tell by the ears."

She grinned back, wiping an errant tear from her

cheek. "Smart ass."

"Once the foal gets up, I'll have a peek."

"Will it get up right away, or does it take a while?"

"Most foals get to their feet within an hour. I'd like to stay long enough to make sure it gets up and feeds properly. Is that okay with you?"

"Yes, of course. Everything's okay with the baby, though, isn't it?"

He watched the tiny black-and-white paint, a carbon copy of its mother, look around the stall with inquisitive bright eyes. "Yeah, it looks like a normal, healthy foal. But I'd like to hang around for a while, just in case."

He needn't have worried. After several shaky attempts, the foal was on its feet and nursing about forty-five minutes after birth. As promised, Cole peeked at the foal's underside.

"We have a boy," he declared.

Lauren clapped her gloved hands silently, whispering, "Well done, Sophie!"

Once the foal had its fill, it lay down on the straw to take a nap. Sophie began to pace back and forth, and shortly after delivered the placenta. Cole examined it carefully for any holes or tears, but it appeared intact. If even a tiny bit of the placenta was left inside her, it could cause a massive infection. He breathed a sigh of relief, knowing his two patients were going to be okay.

"What are you going to name the new foal, Des?" Lauren asked.

"My daughter has been picking out names," he said. "For boys' names, it's a toss-up between Valiant and River. She'll pick one next time she comes to visit. I'll let you know what she decides."

"Yes, please do. I'd love to know what happens with this lovely little fellow," she said.

A short time later, they said their goodbyes to Des. He promised to call Cole if there was any change in either mother or baby that concerned him.

Lauren was quiet on the drive home. She stared pensively out the window, her hands folded neatly in her lap. After pulling into his driveway and turning off the engine, he turned to her in concern.

"You look like you're deep in thought. Anything you want to share?"

She nodded, her brow furrowed. "Actually, there's something I want to ask you."

"What's that?"

"We haven't talked about it, but I'd like to know. Do you want to be in the delivery room for the baby's birth?"

A thrill of emotion coursed through him. "Yes, I want to be there for the baby's birth. I'd like that very much."

She sagged against the truck seat as if relieved by his answer. Her smile seemed to illuminate the cab of his truck. "That's good. I'm glad. I want you to be there."

He caught her hand. "Are you worried about the birth?"

"A little. I'm nervous about the pain, of course, and even though Dr. McKenzie has told me everything is progressing normally, I can't stop worrying that something might go wrong during the delivery." She covered his hand with hers. "You were wonderful today, Cole, so calm and reassuring. Sophie realized she was in good hands. I think I'll need some of your strength when I give birth."

He squeezed her hand, his heart brimming over with love for her. "I'll be there for you, Lauren. No matter what, I'll be with you all through your labor and delivery, every step of the way. You can count on me."

She laid her hand on his cheek. The warmth of her touch sent shivers of heat coursing through his body. "I knew I could. You're my best friend."

Cole caught her hand and kissed the soft palm. Someday, he swore, she'd think of him as more than her friend.

Chapter Eleven

December 15

The Monday morning rush kept Lauren hopping until nearly noon. A steady barrage of calls from clients, along with walk-in traffic, meant she didn't have time for a break until late in the morning. A sudden lull in the action allowed her to make a quick trip to the bathroom, and she seized the opportunity before the phone could ring again.

She washed her hands and headed back to her desk in the reception area. As she rounded a corner, she saw Mia close one of her desk drawers and walk away. *What the hell was that about?*

Lauren immediately went to the cash drawer and recounted the money. Ever since money had begun disappearing, she'd started counting the cash at various intervals throughout the day. She'd done such a count not long before she'd gone to the bathroom. Her records showed that during the morning she'd taken in one hundred and fifty dollars in cash from clients. She counted the money in her drawer, and then counted it again. There was no doubt. She was missing twenty-five dollars. This was the fourth time in the six weeks she'd been at the clinic that it had happened, and this was the largest amount that had gone missing at any one time.

She glanced toward the doorway she'd seen Mia disappear through. This theft had to stop, and it had to stop now.

As she entered a back room where animals recovering after surgery were watched over, she was relieved to find Mia alone. She didn't want an audience for what she was about to say.

There was no point beating around the bush. "I saw you rifling through my desk a minute ago. I recounted the cash drawer and money is missing. If you put the cash back right now and promise never to steal from the clinic again, I won't go to Dr. Waverly and tell him what I saw."

A contemptuous sneer curled Mia's lips. "Billy told me you were crazy, but I didn't realize how crazy until this minute. Take your ridiculous accusations and get the hell out of here."

Lauren stood her ground. "Not till you give back the money."

Mia rose from the stool she'd been sitting at to stand over Lauren. She was several inches taller, and angry. Lauren fought the unease in her gut, unsure if Mia's anger would translate to physical violence. She instinctively laid a protective hand over her belly.

"You're the one with access to the money. You're the one who's responsible for it. If money has gone missing, you're the one who's stealing it. You're trying to pin it on me to cover your ass."

"That's not true! I saw you in my desk!"

"I was looking for a pen." She poked Lauren in the chest with her forefinger. "If you dare tell Dr. Waverly vicious lies about me, you can be sure I'm going to come right back at you. I'd be real worried about my job if I were you. Who are they going to believe? The lowly receptionist they can replace in ten minutes, or the veterinary technician who's had a spotless work record for three years?"

She'd always known Mia was manipulative, but this display told her exactly how far she was prepared to go. This had nothing to do with money. Mia was deliberately trying to discredit her.

"I'm not afraid of you," she said. Lauren's heart raced as she held her ground. She willed her hands to stop shaking. "I know the truth. And Cole knows the truth, too."

Mia gave her an ugly smile. "I'm sure Cole would be so disappointed to learn his saintly little Lauren is nothing but a thief. Imagine how humiliated he'll be when you're fired."

Her stomach lurched, and for a moment she thought she'd be sick, but she made herself look Mia in the eye.

"You may think you can intimidate me into silence, but you can't."

"You don't have proof of anything. It's my word against yours."

She was right. If she was going to prove Mia was stealing from the clinic she'd need iron-clad proof.

Audrey entered the recovery room and looked from her to Mia and back again.

"What's going on?"

"Nothing," Mia said, turning back to her work. "Lauren and I were having a little chat."

"Lauren?" Audrey turned to her, concern in her eyes. "Is that right? Is everything okay here?"

"Yes." She had to find a way to prove Mia was the

thief before she publicly accused her. "Everything's fine."

****

Using his key, Cole entered his mother's apartment, a bag of food balanced on one hip.

"Hi, Mom," he called. "Are you home?"

Ella emerged from the bedroom. "Cole, hi. What are you doing here?"

"Lauren's been busy cooking. She sent some homemade chicken noodle soup and a dozen chocolate chip cookies."

"That was very thoughtful of her," Ella said, taking the bag from him. "Tell her thank you for me."

"I will. Do you need anything? How are you fixed for groceries?"

"I think I have everything I need right now. I was about to make some tea. Would you like some?"

"Sure."

Cole removed his boots and parka at the front door and walked into his mother's small kitchen, past the shrine to his brother on the dining room wall. Though it was compact, the apartment was bright and cheerful, and contained everything his mother needed. Since Ella didn't have a car, the apartment's central location in downtown Masonville meant she could walk almost everywhere she needed to go. The apartment's affordable rent allowed him to cover her expenses without too much strain on his finances. He lived pretty frugally right now, but once the baby came, and if Lauren went back to school, it would be a lot harder to make ends meet.

No matter how difficult, he'd do everything possible to give Lauren the opportunity to finish her education. She deserved it.

Cole sat at the kitchen table, and Ella bustled around her kitchen, putting the kettle on to boil and setting some of the cookies on a plate. He absently ate a cookie while he watched his mother. Was her hair grayer than it had been a few months ago? Aside from Lauren and the baby, she was his last living family, and she was getting older. Despite the many disagreements they'd had over the years, and despite her undisguised favoritism for his brother, he loved his mother. He couldn't help worrying about her. Losing Billy had been hard on her.

She brought two mugs of tea to the table and set one in front of him. "How are Lauren and that soon-to-be grandbaby of mine?"

"They're both doing very well. Lauren's feeling good, and her doctor tells us the pregnancy is progressing normally."

Ella nodded. "I'm glad to hear it." She sipped at her tea, then set down her mug with a sigh. "I only wish Billy was going to be here to see his child."

As usual, it stung to hear her talk about the baby as Billy's child. He wanted to set her straight, claim the baby as his own, but that would only upset her and humiliate Lauren. Instead, he drank his tea and kept his thoughts to himself.

"It's so sad that the baby is going to grow up without a father."

"*I'm* going to be the baby's father, Ma."

Ella waved her hand dismissively. "I meant the child's *real* father. I'm sure you'll be a very good caregiver, but a child, especially a boy, needs his father."

Cole clamped down his anger. "I intend to fill the role of father in every possible way."

"I know you will, Cole. You're a kind person. Look how you took in Lauren in her time of need."

"I care about Lauren. That's why I married her."

"I know you do, and I'm worried about you. I'd hate for you to get hurt. Lauren loved Billy so much. I was shocked that she agreed to marry you, but I know it was because she was pregnant. She was worried about providing for Billy's child. She had no choice but to accept your help. I don't want you to expect too much from her or your relationship. She only lost Billy a short time ago, and you simply can't forget a man like him so quickly."

Cole carefully set his mug on the table instead of hurling it across the room. He hated that he couldn't tell his mother the truth. But he hated even more that she might be right. If Billy was alive, Lauren never would have slept with him, and she certainly wouldn't have married him. She never spoke of Billy, at least not to him, but that didn't mean she didn't miss him and wish he was still with her. Did she regret her most recent marriage?

Would Lauren ever feel anything but friendship for him?

He carefully lifted the mug to his lips and drained it. "I should get back to work, Mom. I've got a couple of calls to make this afternoon."

"Thank you for bringing the food. It was nice to see you."

He hugged her small frame. "It was nice to see you, too."

Cole grabbed his coat and left as fast as he could.

But he couldn't leave behind the doubts his mother had stirred up.

****

Two days after the incident with Mia, the new locks she'd convinced Dr. Waverly to purchase were installed on the cash drawer. Only Lauren and Dr. Waverly had keys, and the drawer was kept locked, even while Lauren was sitting at her desk. She kept the key with her at all times, never leaving it at her desk, and instructed Dr. Waverly to do the same. If she couldn't prove Mia was stealing money, at least she could prevent it.

As a result, the thefts stopped. She hadn't told Dr. Waverly who she suspected, allowing him to believe that someone off the street had done the deed. Mia barely acknowledged her anymore, and that was fine with her. She didn't want anything to do with her either.

She put Mia firmly out of her mind and concentrated on family. Christmas was only eight days away, and she wanted to do something really special this year. She brought up the topic that evening as she and Cole stripped wallpaper from the bedroom that was to be the baby's nursery.

"How do you feel about hosting Christmas dinner this year for our families?"

Cole stopped working to look at her. "Are you sure you want to do that? It'll be a lot of work."

"I want to do it. It'll be fun." She picked at a stubborn piece of wallpaper with her fingernail. Grandma Morris must have pasted the stuff with superglue. "This will be the first time I've had an opportunity to cook a holiday meal for my family. I didn't get to come home for Christmas much the last five years because of Billy's schedule. And it's our first Christmas together. I want to make it special."

"You're sure it's not going to be too much for you?" He grinned at her expanding waistline. "In your delicate condition?"

"I told you before, I'm pregnant, not sick. I'd really like to do this, Cole."

One corner of his mouth turned up in the half grin she found so endearing. "If that's what you want, then that's what we'll do."

"It's going to cost a little extra in groceries," she warned. "We'll need to buy a turkey and all the fixings. Are you okay with that?"

"Lauren." He put down the scraper he'd been using for the wallpaper and reached for her hand. "It's okay. We're far from rich, but we can afford to host Christmas dinner. You know that. You're the one who does the books for the clinic. You even balance my checkbook. Thanks for that, by the way. I can never get anything to balance."

"You're welcome," she said absently. It was such a relief not to fight about finances. Billy had made a big deal about money, especially any time she wanted to spend some of it on her family, or go home for holidays. Cole was generous and open with money. He didn't try to hide anything from her, and he shared what he had, not only with her but with his mother. Billy had loved his parents, in his own way, but his attitude toward money was selfish. What was his was his. She wished Ella would give Cole credit for the generosity he'd shown her.

"Okay, it's settled. We'll host Christmas dinner. You'd better tell your mother about your plans. She might have already started cooking."

"You're right. I should call her. And your mom, too." As she looked up into Cole's face, happiness filled her heart. How incredibly lucky she was to have him in her life. "Thank you."

She stood on her tiptoes to kiss his cheek, bracing herself with her hands against his chest. His arms closed around her, holding her securely against him, her pregnant belly squeezed between them. Cole's dark eyes sparkled with desire. He lowered his mouth to hers, and Lauren shivered in anticipation of his kiss. His lips touched hers, and the taste of him was even sweeter than she remembered. She opened eagerly to him, and he plundered her mouth, his tongue making love to hers. A complex mix of sensations rippled through her body—excitement, pleasure, anticipation. She wanted him. She wanted him with a fervor that bordered on insanity. It had been several days since their wedding, and still they slept in separate bedrooms. Why wouldn't he sleep with her?

They broke the kiss, both of them panting. Lauren gripped his shoulders, holding tightly to him. She had to tell him how much she needed him before she lost her nerve.

"Cole, I—"

Lauren sucked in a breath as a movement in her lower abdomen made her forget everything but the tiny being growing inside her.

Cole held her by her shoulders, his fingers pressing into her flesh. His face paled, and his eyes held a touch of fear, the desire that had burned brightly in them only a minute ago now gone.

"What's wrong? Are you in pain?"

"No, no." She grabbed his hand and placed it on her stomach, covering it with her own. "The baby moved. I thought I felt something earlier, but this was definitely movement."

Another tiny ripple streamed through her belly. Cole's eyes grew wide, his mouth forming an O.

"My God! That's the baby?"

"Yes. Our baby is moving."

He splayed his hand possessively over her stomach and kissed the top of her hair.

"It makes everything real, doesn't it?"

"Yes, it does." She'd known for the last few months she was going to have a baby, but until today it had been something of an abstract concept. Today it became a reality.

He chuckled as he rubbed his hand over her belly. "Hey, baby. Can't wait to meet you in only a little over four more months. How about giving Daddy another little kick? You can do it."

"I think she's gone back to sleep," Lauren said with a smile. "I'll let you know as soon as she wakes up."

"She?"

"It's simply a pronoun. I can't keep calling her 'it.'"

"I suppose not."

Cole kissed her hair one last time, then picked up his wallpaper scraper again.

"I think that was my cue to hustle to get this bedroom ready. Those four months are going to fly by real fast."

Lauren picked up her own scraper. She was thrilled by her baby's first movements, but she wished she'd had the chance to really talk to Cole. She was so confused. His kiss told her one thing, but still he wouldn't touch her.

What did she have to do to make her husband want her?

****

Lauren put her feet up on an extra chair and dunked a tea bag into a cup of hot water. Audrey had volunteered to watch the front desk for a few minutes so she could take a break. The staff break room wasn't exactly luxury accommodation, but it was clean, and the chairs were comfortable. She removed the tea bag, setting it in a small saucer, and opened a small baggie of cookies. An overwhelming craving for chocolate had prompted her to bake the double chocolate chip cookies the previous evening. If she didn't watch her intake of sweets, losing the weight after the baby was born was going to be difficult. But she'd been so good about eating her veggies. A couple of cookies weren't going to kill her.

She bit into one and sighed, her taste buds singing the "Halleluiah Chorus" as they found nirvana. Savoring the chocolate goodness, she closed her eyes and chewed, allowing a smile of pure bliss to curve her lips.

"Who needs sex if you can get off on chocolate? Do you look like that when you make love to your husband?"

Mia's sarcastic voice shattered Lauren's pleasant chocolate-induced buzz. She sat up straight and put her feet on the floor.

"Are you here for a reason, or merely to annoy me?" she said.

"I'm here for my break, of course." She poured herself a cup of coffee and brought it to Lauren's table. She turned up her nose at her cookies. "Are you sure you should be eating stuff like that? I mean, really, you're getting huge."

"It's called pregnancy, Mia."

She had been gaining weight, and although Dr. McKenzie said her weight gain was normal, she knew it wasn't all baby weight. She finished the half-eaten cookie in her hand, not wanting to give Mia the satisfaction of knowing her jab had rattled her. But she left the other cookie in the bag.

"Are you sure you're not having twins? You certainly look big enough to be."

"I'm not having twins." She got up from her chair and dumped her untouched tea down the sink. So much for her nice relaxing break.

"Billy didn't like fat women," Mia continued. "We used to laugh at some of the fat cows at the hockey rink." She tilted her head to one side. "Is Cole more forgiving? What does he say about all the weight you've gained? Does it turn him off?"

Lauren made her way to the door. "Goodbye, Mia."

"I'm curious, Lauren. Which brother do you think is the better lover?"

Lauren paused with her hand on the door, her body vibrating. She wanted to shout at Mia to shut up and leave her alone, to tell her what a miserable, horrible person she was. But she'd likely start crying, and Mia would know she'd gotten the better of her. Instead she turned to her with a smile.

"Cole tells me every day how beautiful I am, and his opinion is the only one that matters to me. He has no problem with my weight. No problem at all."

Holding her head high, she walked out the break room door. She'd seen Mia's frown, and she hoped that meant she thought they were making out like rabbits every night.

But by the time she got back to her desk and shooed away a suspicious Audrey, she was shaking. Despite her show of bravado, Mia's words had succeeded in shattering her already shaky confidence. Maybe the weight she'd gained was the reason Cole wouldn't make love to her. Perhaps he no longer found her attractive.

She told herself she was being ridiculous. Each time Cole kissed her, they both went up in flames. Surely that meant he still wanted her. Or had she been deluding herself all along? Was the one time they'd made love simply an aberration brought on by the shock of Billy's death?

The phone rang. Lauren concentrated on breathing, pushing back the tears that wanted to fall. She wouldn't cry at work, and she certainly wouldn't permit Mia to know she'd hurt her.

Why did he always tell her how beautiful she was if he didn't mean it? Would Cole want her after the baby was born and she lost the weight? If he didn't, their marriage was doomed.

Lauren inhaled deeply and answered the phone.

"Good morning. Masonville Veterinary Clinic. How can I help you?"

****

On Christmas morning, Cole sipped his coffee while he watched Lauren bustle around the kitchen, humming happily to herself. The aroma of turkey roasting in the oven, along with the sweet and tangy smell of cranberry sauce cooking on the stovetop, smelled like holidays and family. He was transported to Christmases past, when his grandmother presided over this same kitchen. There'd always been a lot of laughter and too much food; his dad always joked about needing to buy pants in a size larger the day after Christmas. He'd loved the holidays as a kid because his family had been together.

Now most of them were gone. Last Christmas he and his mother had had a solitary meal together on Christmas Day, Ella expressing her disappointment that Billy and Lauren were unable to come home because Billy had a game the next day. The holiday had been very lonely.

But now he was married to Lauren, and Christmas had taken on a whole new meaning. With her lovely hair pulled back into a ponytail, and his grandmother's pink flowered apron tied around her expanding waist, she was more beautiful than ever. His wife grew more beautiful with each passing day.

His wife. Sometimes he could scarcely believe she'd agreed to marry him. He was so lucky to have her in his life, to soon be having a child with her. But his joy was tempered with the knowledge that if his brother hadn't died, she wouldn't be living with him. She'd still be with him.

"Do you need me to do anything else?" he asked, pushing the disquieting thought away. He wouldn't let anything distract him from enjoying this day with her.

"I think we've got things covered for now. We should be ready to serve dinner at twelve-thirty. Charlotte will be able to spend some time with us before she has to go to work at three," she said with a smile. "Thank you for everything you've done. You've peeled potatoes and carrots, set the table, swept the kitchen floor, washed the dishes. I couldn't have asked for a better assistant."

"I live to serve." He held out his hand. "Come sit down and rest for a bit. You're going to have a busy day."

She grasped his hand and allowed him to tug her toward him, laughing as he pulled her onto his lap.

"I'm too heavy, Cole. You're going to lose all the feeling in your legs."

"Don't be ridiculous." He held her closer. "You're as light as a feather."

"You're such a liar. But thank you for that." She paused a moment. "You know I'm not always going to be this weight, right? Once the baby's born, I'll get back to my pre-pregnancy shape. Hopefully."

He wasn't sure where this conversation was going. "I'm sure you will."

"Does it bother you that I'm getting so big, that I've gained so much weight?"

He looked into her green eyes and saw she was serious. "Of course it doesn't bother me. It means you're having a healthy baby. *My* baby."

"Really?"

"Yeah, really. Sweetheart, I know it must be hard for you with all the changes your body's going through. I wish you could understand how beautiful I think you are. You're beautiful now, and I'll still think you're beautiful once we're old and gray and rocking our chairs in the nursing home."

She searched his eyes before resting her head

against his shoulder and snuggling closer. Cole pulled another chair towards them so she could put up her feet. He buried his face in her fragrant hair, the scent reminding him of the coconut cookies she'd baked a couple of days ago. She was soft and warm and beautiful.

How could she not know that every time he looked at her he was blown away by her beauty? His chest tightened, and he could barely get air into his lungs when she smiled at him. How could she not know that he'd crawl five miles on his hands and knees for one touch of her hand?

How could she not feel his love?

"So what did you get me for Christmas?"

The abrupt change in conversation made him laugh. "You're going to have to wait and see."

"You're not even going to give me a hint?"

"Nope."

She sighed dramatically. "Spoilsport. I got something for you. Actually, I got a few somethings for you, but I wanted to give you one present before everyone gets here."

"Oh, really? What is it?"

"I'll show you. Can you help me up?"

He helped her to her feet, and she went to one of the kitchen drawers and pulled out a small, flat package wrapped in Christmas paper and tied with red satin ribbon. Returning to stand in front of him, she held it out, looking shy and unsure.

"Merry Christmas, Cole."

He tugged on her wrist, bringing her closer. "Come here. You can help me open it."

She sat on his lap once more, and he put his arms

around her, holding her securely. Lauren removed the ribbon and tore open the paper to reveal the back of a picture frame. She held it against her pregnant belly for a minute, not turning it over.

"Remember about a week ago I had an ultrasound at the hospital in Bismarck?"

"Yeah, of course. I wanted to be there, but I had an emergency. You told me everything was progressing normally."

"That's right, it is. But the ultrasound was also able to determine the sex of the baby. Do you want to know? Or would you rather be surprised?"

Cole's heart nearly stopped, and for a moment he was too choked with emotion to speak. He stared at the picture frame in her hands.

"I want to know."

"Okay."

She turned the frame over. It was a black-and-white ultrasound picture, the baby lying suspended inside Lauren's womb. It wasn't clear to him from this picture whether he was looking at a boy or a girl.

Lauren removed her hand, revealing the part of the picture frame she'd been covering. 'Daddy's Little Girl' was stenciled into the pewter.

"A girl," he breathed. Tears stung his eyes. "We're having a girl."

"Yes. Are you happy it's a girl?"

"Lauren." He tightened his hold on her, burying his face against her sweet-smelling neck. "I couldn't be happier. We're having a girl!"

She laughed and wound her arm around his neck. They held each other, and Cole savored the moment. He and Lauren were having a baby girl. It was a wonderful miracle.

Daddy's little girl.

Was that the reason she'd wanted to tell him the news in private? Because she didn't want anyone else to see the picture frame and realize he was the baby's father?

He hated himself for having doubts and ruining this moment of joy. But no matter how much he loved Lauren, he'd always second guess her motives, always wonder about her feelings.

A feeling of loneliness settled on his heart. Maybe he'd always feel alone in this marriage.

Chapter Twelve

December 25

Christmas dinner was a huge success. Lauren's mother had insisted on bringing a couple of homemade apple and pumpkin pies for dessert, Charlotte brought rolls from her favorite bakery in Bismarck, and Garrett brought wine, along with sparkling grape juice for her. Even Ella got into the spirit by bringing a salad. Lauren was happy. It was so wonderful to cook a meal for her family and to have everyone together.

After dinner Cole insisted she put her feet up in the living room while he and Charlotte and Garrett cleaned up and washed the dishes. After they finished, Charlotte began pulling presents from under the tree and passing them around. Her family had brought all their gifts with them so they could open them together.

Lauren laughed at the frilly apron Charlotte had bought her, and marveled at the lovely earrings from Garrett, surprised that the apron came from her sister and the earrings from her brother instead of the other way around. Her parents gave her a beautiful set of china, and Ella's gift was a silk scarf. She hugged all of them, loving them and their gifts. She couldn't stop the tears prickling at her eyes.

Garrett groaned. "Oh, no. You're not going to cry again, are you?"

She dabbed at her eyes, laughing through her tears. "Maybe. Deal with it, Garrett."

"Does she do this all the time, Cole?" he asked in disbelief. "Every time I look at her, she's bawling."

Cole pulled her close and kissed her forehead. "She can cry all she likes, as long as they're happy tears."

"In that case, she must be very happy," Garrett said, shaking his head and laughing.

Lauren gave Cole a shy smile. "I have a lot to be happy about."

His dark eyes glowed with an emotion she couldn't name. The smile on his lips made her believe he was as happy as she was about the baby, and about their marriage.

She handed him two of the boxes Charlotte had passed out.

"These are for you. I hope you like them."

He kissed her forehead. "I know I will."

He opened the large, flat box first, pulling out the sweater she'd bought in a yarn store in Bismarck. It was hand-knit, in a fine Merino wool as soft as silk. She'd known on first sight she had to buy it for Cole. The brown wool reminded her of the deep, dark chocolate color of his eyes.

"It's beautiful, Lauren. Thank you."

"You're welcome. It'll help keep you warm on your rounds this winter. Open the other one."

He complied, tearing the Christmas wrapping from the square box. From the bubble wrap he pulled a wood carving of a foal.

"It reminded me of the foal I saw you deliver."

For a moment, he stared at the piece, not speaking. Lauren swallowed, unsure what he was thinking. She fidgeted in her seat.

"If you don't like it, I can get you something else."

He shook his head, taking her hand and squeezing it. "No, don't do that. I like it. I like it a lot. I wasn't expecting…" He shook his head again, this time lifting his head to grin at her. "Thank you. It'll always remind me of you seeing your first foal being born."

Lauren nodded, relieved. It meant so much to her that he liked her gifts. She couldn't say exactly why, only that she wanted him to know how much he meant to her.

"You haven't opened my gift yet," he said, getting to his feet. "I've been hiding it. Didn't want you trying to guess what it was."

"Guessing is half the fun."

"Guessing what this gift is wouldn't be much of a challenge for you."

She watched as he retrieved a small box from his desk in the corner of the living room, and then sat next to her once more. She stared at the little box, wrapped in silver paper with a tiny blue bow, as he held it out to her.

"Merry Christmas, Lauren."

She accepted the box from him, daring to glance into his face. She caught the nervous tick in his jaw. Did he think she wouldn't like his gift?

The truth was she'd love anything he gave her, simply because it came from him.

"Open it, Lauren. The suspense is killing me," Charlotte said.

Lauren laughed. "Okay, okay."

She removed the bow and ripped off the paper, revealing the jeweler's box. A brooch? Earrings, perhaps? She opened the box with trembling hands. A stunning diamond engagement ring sparkled in the satin folds of the box, an engagement ring to match her beautiful wedding ring.

Her breath caught in her throat. “Oh, Cole.”

“I know it’s backward to get your engagement ring after the wedding ring, but I didn’t want you to miss out.” He squeezed her shoulder. “Do you like it? If you don’t, the jeweler said you can choose something else.”

“It’s perfect.”

“Let’s put it on and see how it looks.”

He plucked the ring from the box, and taking her left hand in his, slipped the ring over her wedding band. Lauren stared at her hand, at the beautiful diamonds glittering in the afternoon sunshine. She hadn’t expected this. She’d never had an engagement ring before, though she’d always secretly wanted one. Because of her pregnancy, she and Billy had been married in such a hurry that there hadn’t been time, but even if there had been more time, they didn’t have the money. Later, Billy was more interested in new skates and hockey equipment than in a ring for her. She was sure it had never crossed his mind to buy her an engagement ring in the five years they were married.

But Cole had. The fact that he’d considered her desires, even though she’d never expressed them, meant the world to her. She looked into his face, hoping she could express to him the depth of her gratitude.

“Thank you.”

Tears streamed down her face once more. Cole wiped them away with the pad of his thumb.

“Oh, great. She’s crying again!”

Lauren couldn’t help laughing at Garrett’s

exaggerated groan. Cole held her as she laughed and cried.

This had turned out to be the most wonderful Christmas she'd ever known.

****

The house was quiet after everyone said goodbye. Charlotte was the first to leave since she had to work the evening shift at the hospital. The others went home after turkey sandwiches and leftover pie in the early evening. Cole put his hands behind his head and stretched out on the couch. It had been a fun afternoon of playing cards, board games, and charades, and there had been much laughter. Even his mother seemed to have a good time.

Lauren padded barefoot into the living room, carrying a couple of mugs of herbal tea and wearing her pajamas and dressing gown. Fresh from her bath, she'd pulled her hair from her ponytail and brushed it till it gleamed. Cole's heart constricted. She was so beautiful he couldn't stop staring, couldn't take his eyes off her. He wanted to stand up and tell the world she was his, that he loved her and always would. He wanted to possess her, hold her, make love to her. He wanted to sink deep inside her, to hear her say his name as she climaxed in his arms.

He sat up and breathed a deep, shaky breath. He couldn't push himself on her that way. He'd told her he wanted a real marriage, but she was pregnant. There was no way he'd take the chance of hurting either her or the baby.

Liar. His reasons for staying out of Lauren's bed had little to do with keeping Lauren safe and everything to do with being a coward.

She handed him one of the mugs of herbal tea before sitting next to him on the sofa and tucking her bare feet beneath her.

"I think everyone enjoyed themselves today, don't you?" she said.

"It was a wonderful Christmas." He tenderly tucked her hair behind her ear. "Thank you for making it such a special day for all of us."

She set her mug on the coffee table. "It was my pleasure, truly. It was such a joy to have everyone gathered together in our house." She looked down at her rings, adjusting them with her other hand. "I can't thank you enough. For everything."

"You really like the ring?" He needed to hear her say it.

She lifted her gaze to his, the expression in her green eyes warm and happy. "I love it, Cole. It's exquisite. It means the world to me that you thought to get me an engagement ring."

"You deserve it." He linked his fingers with hers, needing to touch her.

"Would you kiss me, Cole? Please?"

He wrapped his free hand around the back of her neck and drew her closer, his lips gently touching hers. Her scent, a combination of soap and clean, fresh female, intoxicated him. He moaned and dragged her against him. She parted her lips, and he plundered her mouth greedily, sweeping his tongue around her mouth, drinking from her like a man dying of thirst. She responded with boldness of her own, her tongue mating with his in an act of love simulating the real thing. He groaned once more, and ran his hands over her lush breasts, the swell of her belly, her soft bottom. He wanted her like he wanted his next breath. He had to have her.

If he made love to her, would she compare him to his brother, wish she was making love to him? Would she pretend he was Billy? Would he disappoint her?

He couldn't bear to be second best in her eyes. Regretfully, he pulled away from her, holding her at arm's length. He couldn't make love to her with all the doubts rattling around in his head.

Lauren blinked up at him, her eyes glazed. "Cole? What's wrong?"

"Nothing, sweetheart." He kissed her forehead. "It's late. You should get some rest. You've had a busy day."

Confusion and frustration flickered on her face. "I don't understand. The way you kissed me…I thought you wanted me."

"I do, but we can't. I don't want to hurt the baby. You've miscarried before. The two of you mean too much to me."

It was the truth as far as it went. He didn't want to hurt the baby, but he realized at five months pregnant the risk of miscarriage was likely over.

"You won't. I'm past the point of danger now."

"I can't take any chances."

He hated lying to her. But how could he explain his fear that he that wouldn't measure up to his brother? It was humiliating. How would he ever know whether Lauren wanted him or still longed for Billy?

"Will you at least sleep with me?"

He closed his eyes briefly. His body ached for her. It would be torture to lie next to her and not be able to touch her.

"I don't want to disturb your sleep." He gave her a quick hug and kissed her forehead. "Go to bed, sweetheart."

For a moment he thought she would argue, but instead she gave a resigned sigh.

"Good night, Cole."

She turned and walked to the master bedroom with Brady trailing behind her. He held his breath, listening for the sound of the bedroom door closing before finally exhaling. This couldn't go on. What the hell was he going to do?

****

Lauren awoke abruptly from an uneasy sleep, feeling cold and tired and very alone. She'd barely slept in the three days since Christmas. Though the clinic was closed for the holidays, Cole had taken several emergency calls that had kept him away from home for hours at a time. He probably was glad he had to work so he wouldn't have to be alone in the house with her.

She was so confused. Cole had given her the beautiful engagement ring, which made her think he cared about her, yet he still wouldn't come to her bed. Was the ring merely for show, an attempt to convince the world that they really were husband and wife? She dismissed the idea. She'd known Cole for years, and he simply didn't operate that way. But there was a baby on the way. Knowing Cole the way she did, she conceded he'd want to do the honorable thing by his child, even if he had no feelings for her mother.

No, no, it isn't true. He couldn't kiss her the way he had if he didn't feel any attraction for her.

Her head spun. She couldn't take it anymore. She had to do something.

Flipping back the blankets, she swung her legs onto the cold hardwood floor. As usual, the house was an icebox. She grabbed her robe and slid her feet into slippers before quietly opening the bedroom door. Brady lifted his head from the bed where he'd been sleeping next to her and jumped down to follow her.

"Quiet, boy," she whispered.

Lauren's heart pounded as she made her way down the hall toward the guest bedroom, the only sound the *tap tap tap* of the dog's nails on the hardwood floor. Once she reached the door, she turned the knob and opened the door, still unsure exactly what she was doing here. Cole was sprawled across the bed, half the blankets on the floor as if he'd spent a restless night as well. He lay on his back, completely naked, one arm folded across his eyes, and in his sleep he looked vulnerable. Suddenly, he groaned and rolled onto his side as if he were in pain.

Her heart ached for him. If something was bothering him, she wished he'd talk to her about it. The thought crossed her mind that maybe he'd changed his mind about being married to her and he couldn't bring himself to tell her.

She closed her eyes and swallowed. If that was true, it was better to find out now than to live in limbo indefinitely.

Taking off her robe and slippers, she lifted a corner of the blankets and slid into the bed. She snuggled next to Cole, breathing in his scent and luxuriating in the warmth of his body. It was heaven to touch him. She placed a gentle kiss on his shoulder.

"Lauren."

He breathed her name on a sigh, his eyes still

closed. Was he still asleep? She moved even closer, tucking her head beneath his arm and winding one leg over his. She kissed his flat nipple.

His arm came around her as he woke. "What are you doing here?"

He sounded sleepy and disoriented. Lauren sighed at the feeling of being in his arms.

"I need you. I was cold. Can you keep me warm?"

"Come here."

He held her close, wrapping her protectively in his arms. Lauren nuzzled his neck, loving his scent, his warmth, the feeling of his bare skin against hers. She kissed the line of his jaw, letting her lips linger against his skin, tasting him with her tongue.

With a groan, he dipped his head and captured her mouth in a searing kiss, his tongue plundering her mouth. His erection pushed against her belly, and she silently rejoiced. He wanted her, too.

Her body responded with shudders of desire as dampness pooled between her legs. She ran her hands over his back, his buttocks, his thighs, loving the feel of his hot flesh. Heat rose inside her, scalding her. She wanted him so much, wanted him inside her now.

Lauren slipped a hand between them to stroke his arousal, grasping him gently. His flesh was hot and silky against her skin, exciting her even more.

With a groan, Cole twisted away from her.

"What are you doing?" he said.

"Isn't it obvious? I'm touching you. I want to make love to you."

He flipped back the blanket and sat on the edge of the bed, his face turned away from her so she couldn't see his expression. "It's not a good idea."

"Why?"

She heard the desperation and pleading in her voice. Why was he doing this to her, to them? She was afraid she already had the answer.

"I can't, Lauren. I'm sorry. If anything happened to the baby…I'd never forgive myself."

"That's not the only reason, is it?"

He turned sharply to look at her. "What do you mean?"

"You don't want me. I've gained weight, and you're not attracted to me anymore." She hated the tremor in her voice, and the tears that constantly hovered, waiting to fall.

"No, baby, that's not true."

He crawled across the bed to reach her, taking her hand and placing it on his erection. "Does that feel like I don't want you? I've been in a constant state of arousal for months, ever since our child was conceived. It gets worse every day because you get more beautiful every day."

She clung desperately to his words. Cole had never lied to her, so if he said she was beautiful, it must be true, even if she didn't see it herself. "If you feel that way, why won't you make love to me?"

He dropped her hand looked away. In the semi-darkness she could see him swallow. "Because I'm scared."

"You're really that worried about losing the baby?"

He gave a brusque nod without looking at her. Emboldened by his words, she reached for him again, desperate to make him understand how much she wanted him, needed him. She ran her finger down the length of his penis, pausing to gather a bead of moisture from the tip and swirl it around the head. Cole groaned, though whether in agony or ecstasy Lauren couldn't tell.

"If I prove to you that there's no danger, will you promise to make love to me?"

"How will you prove it?" He croaked out the words, and she smiled, knowing she wasn't playing fair since she still held him in her hand.

"We'll see Dr. McKenzie together. I trust him. If he says it's all right to have sex, we'll know it's safe." She grasped him a little tighter. "Is it a deal?"

"Yes," he breathed.

"Good. But that could take a day or two. In the meantime, I think there's a little something I can do for both of us."

She pushed him back against the pillows, and positioned herself on her knees between his legs. Once more she gently clasped him in her hand.

"Lauren, what are you doing?" His voice was shaky and wracked with passion.

"Shh, sweetheart."

She lowered her head and kissed the tip of his penis, then licked the moisture that dripped off the end. It tasted salty on her tongue. She licked his entire length, placing little kisses around the base. He groaned once more, lifting his hips to give her better access.

"My God, Lauren!"

The passion in his voice made her feel powerful and bold. She guided him into her mouth, swirling her tongue around his shaft, sucking, licking. Little by little she took him deeper. Cole made inarticulate sounds in his throat, telling her how much he needed this, needed her. The sounds went straight to her womb, and she teetered on the edge of her own orgasm. Reaching one hand inside her panties, she touched herself, while at the same time taking Cole even deeper into her mouth.

With a strangled cry, he came in her mouth. She took everything he had to give, loving the taste of him. She orgasmed as well, her body writhing with pleasure. Sweet release flowed through her body.

Eventually, their breathing returned to normal. Cole sat up and reached for her.

"Come here, sweetheart."

She willingly slipped into his arms. He held her tightly for a moment, then laid her down against the pillow and carefully covered her with the scattered blankets. He said nothing more, but caressed her face, his thumb drawing gentle circles beneath her eye. The expression in his eyes made her feel cherished.

Loved.

Cole had never spoken of love. Neither had she. She'd always loved him as a friend, but was she *in love* with him? Being in love was a frightening possibility, leaving her vulnerable and open to hurt. She'd been in love with Billy and it had brought her a lot of pain.

Snuggling against him, she dismissed the thought. For the moment she was happy to simply be in her husband's bed.

****

The next morning the sound of the alarm on his cell phone woke Cole from the first good sleep he'd had in weeks. He reached over and turned off the alarm, not wanting to wake Lauren. She slept peacefully next to him, her hand resting on his chest. Tenderness swamped him as he looked into her lovely, sleeping face. God, he loved her. He couldn't believe what they'd done last night, couldn't believe what she'd been willing to do. The thought of Lauren's mouth around him caused him to instantly harden. He ached with wanting her.

Had she pleasured Billy that way?

Stop it! He wished he could banish the jealous notions from his head, but he couldn't stop thinking about his brother making love to Lauren.

Had she thought of Billy as she was making love to him last night?

He stifled a groan and carefully swung his legs over the side of the bed. This was getting him nowhere. Quietly, he grabbed some clothes and left the room. A lukewarm shower helped cool his heated blood. By the time he returned to the guest room, Lauren was dressed for work. Her smile lit up her face as he opened the door.

"Good morning. Did you sleep well?" she asked.

"Yeah, I slept great. How about you?"

"I had a wonderful sleep. It's the first time I've been really warm since I moved into this house. Sleeping with you is like having a nice, cozy furnace in my bed."

"Good, that's good." He grabbed a brush from the dresser and pulled it through his hair, trying not to meet her eyes in the mirror.

"I think it's going to be busy at work today."

"Yeah." He looked everywhere but at her.

"I hope it doesn't snow."

"Yeah." Why couldn't he talk to her?

"Cole? Are you sorry?"

Her words were so softly spoken he almost didn't hear them. He turned to face her. Her smile was gone, her face pale. He couldn't let her think that last night didn't matter to him, that it hadn't been amazing. He sat next to her on the bed and gripped her hand.

"The last thing I am is sorry."

She looked down at their joined hands. "You're sure you aren't surprised, or…disgusted by what I did?"

"No! Lauren, look at me."

Reluctantly, she lifted her gaze to his. He squeezed her hands, searching for words to express his feelings. "Last night was incredible. *You* were incredible."

"Then why are you so different this morning, so cold?"

"I don't mean to be. I'm sorry." He opted for a half-truth. "You're the most amazing woman I've ever known. You throw me off-kilter, turn my world upside down. I guess I'm trying to get my bearings."

"Does that mean you'll still come with me to see Dr. McKenzie?"

He kissed her forehead, letting his lips linger against her soft skin. His heart soared at the knowledge she wanted to make love with him and was eager to prove to him that it was safe for the baby. That had to mean something. "Of course."

"And you'll abide by whatever he says?"

"If he says there's no danger in having sex, I won't worry about it anymore."

"Promise?"

He raised their joined hands and kissed her knuckles. "Promise."

"I want us to be a real family, Cole. You and me and the baby. I want that more than anything I've ever wanted in my life. And that means we share our lives, and our bodies, as husband and wife."

He wished he could tell her the truth about his feelings. He wished he could speak openly about playing second fiddle to Billy. Hell, he'd never even told her how much he loved her. He was afraid if she understood the depth of his jealousies and insecurities, if she knew he'd been in love with her, lusted after her, the entire time she was married to Billy, she'd run away as quickly as she could. And he wouldn't blame her.

If he wanted Lauren in his life, he'd have to put aside any doubts about the past. He had to make himself forget that she'd once chosen his brother over him.

"I want us to be a family, too. Very much."

Chapter Thirteen

December 29

Lauren phoned Dr. McKenzie's office as soon as she got to work and was able to make an appointment for that morning. She and Cole slipped away from the clinic shortly before eleven. Snow fell in fat, wet flakes and accumulated on the streets. When they reached the family health clinic, Cole helped her from his truck and kept an arm around her waist to steady her on the icy sidewalk. She smiled gratefully at him. He always made her feel safe and cared for.

After some initial blood and urine work, Dr. McKenzie performed an internal exam. Lauren dressed and joined Cole in the doctor's office, reaching for her husband's hand as soon as she sat next to him. She had to make Cole understand that he had nothing to worry about. But a feeling in the pit of her stomach told her the health of the baby wasn't his only concern.

He's sorry he married you, Lauren.

She'd trapped him into this marriage, even though it had been his idea. If she hadn't fallen apart after Billy's funeral, if they hadn't had sex, perhaps the friendship they'd always shared would have grown naturally over time into something more intimate.

Yet how could she regret having the baby she'd always wanted? She'd do everything she could to be a good wife to Cole, and to protect the family they were creating.

Dr. McKenzie joined them in his office. "You're doing very well, Lauren. The baby's size is exactly what we'd expect at this time. Was there something bothering you that prompted you to make this appointment?"

"We've been concerned about the safety of making love. Because I had two miscarriages before, Cole and I were worried that having sex might trigger another one."

"The miscarriages you experienced were in the early weeks of your pregnancies and were likely the result of problems with the fetus rather than anything you did or didn't do. You're in your second trimester now, and everything is progressing normally. As long as you both want sex, and Lauren can be comfortable, there's no reason not to have it."

"So there's no way I can hurt the baby?" Cole asked.

"No. The baby is protected by the amniotic fluid in the uterus and by the strong muscles of the uterus itself, so there's no danger. As Lauren gets bigger, you might want to experiment with positions that take the weight off her abdomen and allow her to control the depth of penetration. Mostly, it's about doing what feels good. Some women find their sexual desire is heightened during pregnancy, and others find it diminished. Both are absolutely normal."

"What about oral sex? Is it safe?" Lauren could feel her cheeks heat with her blush as she asked the question.

"Yes," Dr. McKenzie said with a nod. "Licking

and kissing is perfectly all right. And there are other ways to be intimate without having sex, if that becomes too uncomfortable. You can try cuddling or massage, any skin-to-skin contact that feels good and brings you closer together physically and emotionally."

It seemed a little strange to be talking about sex in such a clinical, unemotional way, but Dr. McKenzie's kind, matter-of-fact manner made it easier to ask the questions they needed answered. If it convinced Cole to have sex with her, she'd ask any number of embarrassing questions.

Having sex with Cole had become her primary goal. God, she ached for him. The strength of her desire shocked her. She found herself daydreaming about touching him, stroking him, pleasuring him. The thought of him touching her sensitive breasts, of being inside her, almost made her spontaneously orgasm. She'd never been such a sex fiend before. In fact, in the last months of their marriage, she hadn't wanted Billy to touch her at all.

Was this heightened desire only a by-product of her pregnancy, or was there something about Cole that made her want him so badly?

"Have I set your minds at ease?" Dr. McKenzie asked. "Do you have any more questions?"

Lauren looked at Cole and squeezed his hand. "I think you've answered all my questions. What about you, Cole?"

"Yes, I think so."

"Good. If you think of anything else, don't hesitate to call me. The most important thing to do is to keep the lines of communication open between you. Talk to each other, about sex and how you feel about it, about your upcoming role as new parents, and about your relationship. As long as you're honest about your feelings, your relationship will be able to withstand all the changes that having a baby will bring into your lives."

She hadn't been totally honest with Cole. She'd never told him the truth about her marriage to Billy, hadn't been able to bring herself to. It was humiliating to speak of the way Billy had cheated on her. And no matter what he'd done, Billy was still Cole's brother. She didn't want to ruin his memories of him.

They thanked the doctor and left his office, venturing outside into the growing storm once more. The drive back to the clinic was slow. Visibility was reduced to a few yards in front of the truck, and treacherous ruts had formed on the roads. Lauren wanted to talk to Cole about what the doctor had told them, but he was too preoccupied with driving. Once they reached the clinic, she'd take him aside for a moment to talk. The storm meant many of their clients would likely cancel their appointments for the afternoon, giving them plenty of time.

Audrey met them as soon as they walked through the front doors of the clinic. "We just got a call from Prairie Pride Dairy farm. Tim Reed says he's got a pneumonia outbreak in his herd. He thinks it came from a couple of new cows he bought in Minnesota. His cattle need antibiotics immediately."

Cole sighed and nodded. "I'll get my meds together."

Lauren put her hand on his arm. "You're going now, in this storm?"

"I have to. If we don't treat the infected cattle

immediately, it'll spread to the rest of the herd. The dairy could lose production and possibly some animals."

"But the dairy is at least ten miles from town."

He rubbed her arm as if he were trying to soothe her. "I know, but I've got four-wheel drive on the truck. I'll be fine."

"I'll come with you. I can help you."

"No. Absolutely not." His tone told her he wasn't going to budge this time. "I'll feel much better if I know you're safe here at the clinic. Audrey, if I'm not back by five, can you give Lauren a ride home?"

"Don't worry, Cole. I'll make sure she gets home safely."

"Thanks." He turned to Lauren, taking her shoulders between his hands and kneading softly. "Don't worry, sweetheart. I'll be back before you know it."

In the weeks she'd been working at the clinic, he'd never called her sweetheart in front of their colleagues or engaged in any sort of public display of affection. That he did now made a lump form in her throat. She stepped into his arms and held him tightly for a minute.

"I'll be waiting for you," she whispered in his ear.

When she stepped back, his eyes glittered with passion. He was remembering his promise to make love to her if they got the green light. *Good.* Hopefully that would give him added incentive to finish his work quickly and rush home to her.

****

Where was he? Lauren paced the living room, stopping to peer through the front window yet again, hoping to see the headlights of Cole's truck shining through the darkness. But all remained dark, with no sign of him. He should have been home by now. When she'd phoned Tim Reed at the dairy farm, he'd told her Cole finished with the inoculations and left about thirty minutes previously. That had been over an hour ago.

She tried his cell phone and got the same message she'd received for the past hour. *The customer is away from their cell phone. Please call back later.*

Lauren was sick with worry, but she pushed down her fears so she could think. He had to be stuck somewhere on the road between the dairy farm and Masonville. But why wasn't he answering his phone? Surely there was cell phone coverage ten miles from town. The only good news was that the snow had stopped falling, though the wind continued to whip it into frothy drifts that snaked across the driveway.

Cole was in trouble. She could feel it. She hated to drag her brother out on a night like this, but he was the only person she could think of who could help her. She punched Garrett's number into her phone and sighed with relief when he answered after several rings.

"Hey, Lauren. What's up?" Garrett sounded disoriented, his voice slurred as if he'd just woken.

"I'm sorry to bother you, but I've got trouble." She filled him in on the situation.

"The dairy's not far from here." Garrett was living with their parents on the farm until he got his own place. "I'll go out on my snowmobile and check for Cole's truck."

A sob escaped Lauren's mouth at his words. "Thank you."

"Hey, don't cry. I'll find him, okay?"

She did her best to hold back her tears. "Okay. Be

safe. I love you, Garrett."

"I love you, too. I'll call you as soon as I know something."

"Okay."

Time dragged as she waited to hear from Garrett, giving her vivid imagination the opportunity to come up with horrible scenarios. What if Cole's truck had gotten stuck and he decided to walk for help? What if he got disoriented in the snowstorm and froze? What if he stayed in his truck and was overcome by carbon monoxide?

"Stop!" she said out loud, startling the dog, who had been pacing with her. He whined pitifully, her anxiety transferring to him. She'd drive herself, and Brady, stark-raving mad if she kept this up. She couldn't lose Cole. Not now, not with their baby coming in a few months. She needed him.

She loved him.

She rolled that thought around in her mind. *She loved him.* Not only as a friend the way she'd always loved him, but as a husband, a lover. He was a wonderful, kind, compassionate man, and she wanted to spend her life with him. Surely fate wouldn't be so cruel as to take him away from her now.

The phone rang, and Lauren pounced on it before it had a chance to ring twice.

"Garrett?"

"I've got him, Lauren."

She held back her sob of gratitude. "Is he okay?"

"He's cold, but fine. He hit the ditch a couple of miles from the dairy farm. Right now he's dressing in the extra snowmobile suit I brought with me, and then we're heading into town. We should be at your house within a half hour."

"Why didn't he call me? Is there something wrong with his phone?"

Garrett laughed. "Yeah. He forgot to charge it."

Lauren didn't know whether to laugh or cry. She was going to smack her husband as soon as he got home. Right after she kissed him senseless.

True to Garrett's promise, they arrived at her front door on his snowmobile about twenty minutes later. Cole entered the house and removed his helmet, his eyes meeting hers. Lauren ran to him with a little cry and threw herself into his arms. He held her tightly, nuzzling her neck.

"It's okay, sweetheart. I'm home now. Thanks for calling out the cavalry."

She leaned back to look at him through her tears, swatting him on the shoulder.

"Don't ever leave on a call without charging your phone. I was worried sick when I couldn't reach you."

"I'm sorry, baby."

He kissed her tenderly, wiping away the tears on her cheeks. "It's all right now."

She nodded, clinging to him. She couldn't stop crying. All she could think was that she loved him and she could have lost him.

Garrett cleared his throat. "I'll be going now. I'll talk to you soon."

Cole shook his hand, keeping one arm around Lauren. "Thanks, Garrett. I owe you."

"Are you sure you want to go out there in this weather?" Lauren asked, as she wiped fresh tears from her eyes. "Why don't you stay until the morning?"

"I'll be fine. I think the two of you need some

privacy," he said with a grin.

Lauren kissed her brother's cheek, surprised by the smell of alcohol on his breath. She grasped his arm. "You're sure you don't want to stay?"

"I'm sure."

"Call me as soon as you get home, okay?"

"Okay. See you later."

He slipped out the door, and Lauren went to the window to watch him leave. Garrett straddled the snowmobile and it roared to life. In a few moments, her brother and the machine disappeared into the darkness, the sound of the engine gradually fading. Something was going on with him. First chance she got, she'd have a private conversation with Garrett.

"Lauren?"

She turned to Cole, suddenly feeling shy and unsure. What if he didn't have the same feelings for her that she'd just discovered she had for him?

She lifted her gaze to his. "Would you like something to eat? I can make you something."

"No, thanks, not right now." He stepped close and brushed her hair from her face. "You said you'd be waiting for me."

"I was. I am."

He cupped her cheek with his work-roughened hand. "I thought about you every minute I was stuck in that ditch. I can't tell you how frustrated I was not to be with you. I couldn't even talk to you on the phone. I'm sorry I worried you."

Her heart sang at his words. "I know you are."

"All I could think about was being with you, in our bed, making love. That's all I want. Will you come to bed with me, Lauren?"

"Yes. Oh, yes."

She accepted his outstretched hand and followed him to the master bedroom, anticipation in her every step. Carefully he undressed her until she stood in front of him completely naked. He tenderly caressed her pregnant belly, his gaze never leaving hers.

"You're so beautiful."

She unbuttoned his shirt, kissing his bare skin. "So are you."

He grunted. "There's nothing special about me."

Tilting her head, she examined his expression. Did he really believe that? She pushed his open shirt down his shoulders and let it fall to the floor. "You're wrong. You're very special and very beautiful." She skimmed her hands over the hard muscles of his shoulders and chest, the touch of his skin arousing her even more. "When you hold me, I feel the strength in your body, the power, yet you're always so gentle, and you make me feel so safe."

He clutched her shoulders. "And when I kiss you? What do you feel?"

"I feel like the fourth of July," she said with a grin. "Fireworks and explosions and lights of every color flashing behind my eyes. I have to tell you, Cole, you're an amazing kisser."

He laughed. "Really?"

"Really." She closed the space between them, winding her arms around his neck and pressing her naked breasts against his bare chest. She could feel his erection strain against his jeans.

It made her feel powerful to know he wanted her so much.

"Kiss me, Cole. Let's pretend it's the fourth of

July."

He lowered his head to touch his lips to hers. They were soft and warm, and when he opened his mouth for her, he tasted of the sweetest honey. She drank greedily, like a woman dying of thirst in a barren desert.

But it wasn't enough. Not nearly enough.

He scooped her into his arms and carefully laid her on the bed before stripping off the remainder of his clothes. In the soft glow of the bedroom lamps she watched the play of light on the muscles of his shoulders, the proud thrust of his erection. How could such power be so gentle at the same time?

"Like I said. You're beautiful, Cole."

For a second he silently stared at her. Then he joined her on the bed, stretching out beside her. His gaze never left her face.

"Thank you."

His eyes glowed with an emotion she couldn't name. She lifted his hand and placed it on her breast, needing him to touch her, needing him to know how much she loved him.

Without another word he straddled her hips, keeping all his weight on his arms. He teased the opening of her body with his arousal, driving her half mad with desire. When he took her breast into his mouth, sucking and licking the distended nipple, she threw back her head and arched her back, her body trembling.

"Please Cole. I need you."

He didn't make her wait. He slipped easily inside her, filling her, stretching her. But she sensed he was holding back, being careful not to push too far or too deep.

She didn't want him to hold back. She wanted all of him, body and soul. She wanted him to feel her love. With a cry of frustration, she lifted her hips, while at the same time pushing her hands against his buttocks to bring him closer.

"Please, please," she begged, her head thrashing back and forth on the pillow, her eyes closed.

"Look at me, Lauren."

She blinked up at him, her eyes slowly focusing on his face.

"I want to see your face while I make love to you. I want you to look at me. I want you to know—"

"What?" she whispered when he didn't finish. "What do you want me to know?"

"That it's me inside you."

She didn't know what to say to that. How could he not know how special he was to her? That he was the only man she wanted? She wished he'd share his thoughts with her, his heart. All she could do was to try to communicate her feelings, and her love.

Caressing his face, she whispered, "Only you."

His dark eyes glittered with emotion. With his arms still holding his weight, he thrust into her.

"Am I hurting you?"

She shook her head. "No, God, no. Don't stop, please."

A satisfied grin spread across his face. "Whatever you say, sweetheart."

He withdrew, then thrust again. Over and over, deeper and deeper. Lauren stayed with him, her gaze steady on his face, unable to stop the incoherent sounds of passion that escaped from her parted lips. She clutched at his shoulders, his back, his buttocks, anywhere she could reach. Needing to touch him, needing him closer.

She began to quiver, then her body bowed as her release came. She stared into his eyes.

"Cole." She didn't know if his whispered name on her lips was a plea or a benediction. She only knew she loved him. "Cole."

His release came then, and she realized he'd been waiting for her. Powerful spasms shook his body, and she wanted to hold him through the storm, but he was still propped on his elbows. Knowing he was trying not to hurt her made her love him even more.

Finally, he collapsed next to her and threw one arm around her, bringing her close. Neither of them spoke; somehow it didn't seem necessary. Lauren laid her head against his chest and let the steady beat of his heart lull her to sleep.

****

Cole held Lauren in his arms while she slept. She was soft and warm, and her hair held the fragrance of flowers. Her right hand rested on his chest, near his heart, as if she needed to assure herself, even in sleep, that he was nearby.

His heart ached to look at her. He'd been a fool to stay away from her bed for so long. She'd gone to a lot of trouble to prove to him there was no danger to the baby in having sex. That had to mean something. The ardent way she'd responded to his touch, to his kisses, told him she wanted him. For the sake of their family, he had to put aside any lingering doubts and concentrate on making her happy.

The phone on the bedside table rang. Cole reached around Lauren to grab it, trying not to wake her.

"Hello," he said quietly.

"Cole, it's Garrett. Can you tell Lauren I'm home, safe and sound?"

"I will. And thanks again."

"No problem."

He carefully set the receiver back on the cradle. Lauren blinked up at him, and her body tensed.

"Do you have to go out on another call?"

"No. That was Garrett, telling you he got home safely. I'm not going anywhere. I couldn't go even if I wanted to. My truck's still in a ditch miles from town, remember?"

"I'm relieved, on both counts." She sighed and snuggled against his chest once more. "I'm glad your truck's still stuck. If you were planning to go out into that snowstorm again, I'd find a way to stop you, even if it meant tying you to this bed."

"That sounds…interesting."

She looked up into his face and laughed. "I was kidding, but hey, if you're into that sort of thing…"

He kissed her laughing mouth, loving the way she wrapped her arms around him, loving the gentle banter between them. They'd always shared a similar sense of humor, laughing at the same jokes and absurdities of life. Billy had often been baffled by the things they found funny.

Cole pulled away from Lauren. He hadn't meant to bring Billy into bed with them, but somehow his brother had wedged himself between them once again.

"Have you eaten?" he asked, hoping to change the direction of his thoughts.

Before she could answer, her stomach rumbled. She chuckled as she laid a hand on her pregnant belly.

"No, I haven't. I think that's Junior Missy's subtle way of telling me it's time."

"Junior Missy? Is that what you're calling the baby now?"

"Until we come up with a proper girl's name, it'll have to do."

Giving their child a name made her even more real. He could hardly believe she'd be born in a few short months. "Come on. I'm starved. I worked up an appetite sitting in that ditch. Let's see what we can find in the kitchen."

He found his discarded jeans on the floor and started pulling them on.

"Wait," Lauren said. She slid to the edge of the bed, the sheet wrapped around her breasts. Reaching out her hand, she touched his right hip. "What is this?"

Cole looked down at his hip where her finger lightly caressed his skin. "That? It's only a birthmark."

"I never noticed it before."

"That's because it's usually hidden under my boxer shorts."

Her grin was mischievous. "Finally, all is revealed." She returned to her examination. "It looks like a map of Italy."

He laughed. "A map of Italy?"

"Sure." She outlined the birthmark with her finger. "It has a shape like a boot, like Italy. Do you think our baby will have a birthmark?"

He pulled up his jeans and fastened them. "I suppose it's a possibility. But it's not a big deal, especially if it's located on a part of her body where the sun doesn't shine, like mine."

She laughed and slid from the bed. "You're right.

In the vast scheme of things, a birthmark is the least of our worries."

After dressing in their discarded clothes, they made their way to the kitchen. Lauren scrambled eggs while Cole toasted whole wheat bread and poured milk for them both.

"Do you have any names for the baby picked out?" he asked.

She pulled a frying pan from a cupboard. "I've mulled over a few names. How about you?"

"To be honest, I haven't given it any thought until now. But she's coming soon. I guess we should be prepared."

"All these changes in your life must have your head spinning."

"We've both gone through some big changes in a short period of time." He gripped her chin gently in his hand and made her look into his face. He wanted her to see the truth in his next words. "I couldn't be happier about having you in my life. And I'm excited that we'll have a daughter together very soon."

She smiled tremulously. "I've been thinking about the name Piper."

"Piper." He said it out loud, testing it on his tongue. It felt good. "I like it."

"Does that mean we've picked a name?"

"I think it does."

"That was way easier than I thought it would be." She laughed and lifted her glass of milk in a toast. "To Piper."

Cole tapped his glass against hers. "To Piper."

Chapter Fourteen

February 20

"Birth partners, it's important to support the mother, both figuratively and literally."

Cole sat on a mat on the floor of the community center in Bismarck, with Lauren sitting in front of him, her back leaning against his chest. They sat in a circle with twenty other pregnant women and their birth partners. Some of the partners were husbands like him, but others were friends, and in a couple of cases, mothers or sisters of the pregnant women. The small hospital in Masonville no longer handled maternity cases. Piper would be born in a hospital in Bismarck, some ten miles from Masonville.

"Sometimes sitting like this on the bed or the floor will feel comfortable for the mother during labor, and at other times she may want to walk. You have to remain flexible, to take your cues from your partner and help her to find a position that's comfortable for her at each stage."

Cole put his arms around Lauren, his hands resting on her belly. He grinned when the baby kicked against his hand.

"Is this comfortable for you?" he whispered in her ear.

She leaned her head against his shoulder. "Yes,

very. You make a good pillow."

"Thanks a lot. I hope I'm useful for more than a back rest."

She looked up at him, all innocence as she wriggled closer to his crotch. "Oh, yes. You're very useful. In fact, I plan to put you to good use as soon as we get home."

His body instantly responded to her words. These days he couldn't touch Lauren, could barely talk to her, without wanting her. Fortunately, the feeling was very mutual. Since they'd been given the green light by Dr. McKenzie, they couldn't keep their hands off each other.

But it was damned embarrassing, not to mention uncomfortable, to get a hard-on in the middle of their prenatal class.

"You're killing me, Lauren. Behave and pay attention to the instructor," he whispered in mock outrage.

Her throaty chuckle only made him harder. She *was* killing him, but what a way to go.

The instructor continued. "Tonight, we're going to talk about a few methods the birth partner can use to help the mother relax during labor. The first is breathing. During labor, the mother is tense and frightened, and the natural tendency is to take fast, shallow breaths. But this doesn't allow enough oxygen for either the mother or the baby, and soon both will become exhausted. The object in labor is to conserve as much energy as we can for later when the mother needs to push. Birth partners, you can help your mother to conserve her energy and help to alleviate some of the pain of contractions by reminding her to breathe. So right now we're going to practice taking deep, calming breaths together. Partners and mothers, I want you to face each other, so you can see each other's face."

Cole positioned himself in front of Lauren. Despite all the kidding between them, he was serious about this class. If there was anything he could do to help her through the birth of their child, he'd do it. The thought of Lauren in pain caused his gut to twist into a knot. He clasped her hands, and she squeezed back in silent communication.

"For a moment, breathe normally. Notice how rhythmic your breathing is. You breathe in, and there's a slight pause before you breathe out. The goal during labor is to keep that rhythm. Don't allow the out-breath to get shorter than the in-breath. If anything, make sure the out-breath is longer.

"Sometimes it's helpful to concentrate on a word or action during breathing exercises. Let's try this one. Think of the word 'relax.' It has two syllables—'re' and 'lax.' As you breathe in, silently say to yourself 're,' and as you exhale, silently say 'lax.' Focus on that word; if your mind wanders away from it, gently steer it back. As you breathe out, try to let any tension flow out of your body along with your breath. Let's try this together."

Cole inhaled, then slowly breathed out, and watched Lauren do the same. He saw her shoulders relax as she expelled her breath.

"Remember to say to yourself 'laaaax' on the out-breath and let everything go. The out-breath is the one to concentrate on because the in-breath will take care of itself. Partners, during labor it's your job to remind the mother to breathe this way. Look into her face and breathe with her during a contraction. She's going to be so focused on the contraction that she's going to forget nearly everything we've talked about here, so it's your job to remember."

They practiced deep breathing for a while before the instructor moved on to the next topic. "Massage has been found to relieve pain and reduce anxiety. It can be very helpful during labor to some mothers. Some find it so beneficial they demand their partners massage them for hours on end. Some mothers don't want to be touched at all. If that's the case, don't take it personally. And dads, if she tells you to go to hell and never come back, don't take that too personally either. Emotions can run a little high."

Everyone laughed, but it was laughter mixed with nervousness. The instructor continued.

"The shoulders hold a lot of tension, so massaging there can relieve stress. Many women experience pain in the lower back. Partners, let's practice this right now. Use the flat of your hand to stroke down one side of her spine. Then use your other hand to stroke down the other side of her spine. Keep one hand in constant contact with her back. Use your whole hand, not solely the heel. This is a comforting form of massage for early labor. You can use a massage oil if you wish."

Cole moved behind Lauren once more. Following the instructions, he ran his hands up and down Lauren's back. She sighed and let her head drop forward.

"That feels wonderful. If you massage my back while I'm in labor, I promise I won't tell you to go to hell."

He chuckled. "It's a deal."

"Partners, in advanced labor, the mother might

need a more vigorous massage. You can use the heel of your hand to massage the base of her spine. You might need to apply a fair bit of pressure to counteract the contractions. Or you can press your thumbs in the dimples of her bottom if that helps. Remember, it's whatever is helpful to the mother."

The instructor showed them how to massage the feet, making sure to use sufficient pressure to keep the massage from being unbearably ticklish. She told them a hand massage could be soothing, especially if the mother was given an epidural. She wouldn't feel her feet in that case, so massaging her hands might be the only option left.

Lauren seemed to enjoy all the massages, and Lord help him, he loved touching her. He hoped she'd be able to tolerate his touch during labor.

"That's it for tonight, everyone. I want you to practice the breathing and massage techniques at home. Next time we'll take a tour of the labor and delivery room at the hospital."

Cole pulled Lauren to her feet and helped her put on her coat. He reached for her hand as they walked out of the community center.

"How do you feel?" he asked.

She hugged his arm. "Very re-laaaaxed. Have I ever told you what wonderful hands you have?"

"No, I don't believe you have."

"Well, I'm telling you now. I think I'm going to need those wonderful hands on me as soon as we get home."

He leaned over to kiss her before helping her into the truck. "Anything for the little mama."

****

"Good morning. Masonville Veterinary Clinic. How can I help you?"

The phone had been particularly busy the past week. Since word had gotten out that Dr. Jamie was interested in treating exotics, business was booming. The local paper had done an article about her, including a picture with her and her Grey Parrot, Hector. The article had circulated widely on the paper's website, and many iguanas, boa constrictors, and lizards, along with their owners, had trooped by Lauren's desk, travelling from all over North Dakota, northern South Dakota, and eastern Montana to see Dr. Jamie. Lauren shivered at the thought of the boa constrictor she'd seen wrapped around the neck of its owner. She'd stick with a dog as a pet. At least she didn't have to worry about Brady strangling her.

She looked up to see Cole approaching her desk. Her heart made a little pitter-pat in her chest at the sight of him. When he smiled at her, her whole being filled with sunshine. She couldn't believe how her life had changed in such a short period of time. Every day she loved him more, and every day he made her a little happier. She only wished she could tell him the depth of her feelings. Every time she tried to speak of the love burning inside her, fear clogged her throat. She didn't understand why she was so afraid, only that she was.

So she'd turned to sex to express her love. She poured her feelings into every caress, every kiss, every thrust. She desperately needed to show him how much he meant to her.

"Hi," Cole said, coming around the desk to kiss her.

She loved the taste of his kiss. "Hi yourself. Did

you need something?"

"Just to see my beautiful wife. I had some time between appointments, and I wanted to see how you were doing."

"I'm great." She lowered her voice to a whisper. "I'll be even better once we get home. I've been thinking about what I want to do with you when I get you alone."

He grinned. "Oh, yeah?"

"Oh, yeah." She tugged on his shirt, bringing him closer. "Get ready, Dr. Walsh."

"Promises, promises."

Cole's kiss sent waves of heat rippling through her body. He swept her mouth with his tongue, demanding a response. She shivered with desire as she touched her tongue to his, boldly imitating the way he possessed her mouth. Cole made her feel powerful, as if she could do anything and didn't need to apologize for it.

"Save some of that for the bedroom, guys."

Mia's sarcastic tone doused Lauren's ardor immediately. She broke their kiss and pulled away, suddenly feeling embarrassed when only a moment ago she'd been invincible. She cursed herself for allowing Mia to take that away from her.

Cole laid his hand on Lauren's shoulder in silent support. "Was there something you wanted, Mia?"

"I needed to give these supply requisitions to Lauren." She put some forms on the desk. "I'm glad to see the two of you having so much fun. After all the tragedy in your lives, you deserve some happiness."

"Thank you. My next appointment will be here any minute. I'll see you later." He brushed a quick kiss across Lauren's lips before walking away.

As soon as he was out of earshot, Mia turned to her with a sly smile. “So how long has it been since Billy died? Seven months? You certainly haven’t wasted any time grieving for him.”

Lauren was sick of the inquisition. “Have you?”

Mia’s smile disappeared. “Billy and I had a very special relationship. I understood him far better than you ever did. He should have married me, not you, but you trapped him with that fake pregnancy.” She gave a bitter, ugly laugh. “We never let a little thing like marriage keep us apart. I gave him what he never got from you.”

Evelyn entered the main reception area and walked up to Lauren’s desk, her gaze darting to Mia, and then Lauren, and back to Mia.

“What’s going on? Are you all right, Lauren?”

Mia jumped in before Lauren could answer. “What a silly question! Of course she’s all right. We were merely chatting about how wonderfully her life has turned around since Billy’s death, and how lucky she is. Well, it’s been nice talking to you, Lauren. I’d better get back to work.”

Lauren released a relieved breath as Mia disappeared into a back room. Beside her, Evelyn snorted derisively. “Chatting, my ass. What did she really want?”

“It was nothing, Ev.” She dredged up a smile for her friend. “But thanks for caring.”

“Watch that one, Lauren. She’s the kind that’ll happily stick a knife in your back when you’re not looking.”

“Don’t worry. I’m well aware.”

Evelyn nodded in satisfaction before going back to

work. Clients of Dr. Waverly's arrived in the reception area with three dogs, and for a few moments Lauren was too busy to think about what Mia had said. But after she'd guided them into an examining room and returned to her desk, the words came back to haunt her.

I gave him what he never got from you.

Had she been such a dismal failure as a wife that Billy needed to look outside their marriage for satisfaction, sexual and otherwise?

No. She'd tried to please him in every way, but nothing she'd done had kept him from cheating. She'd stayed and tried to make their marriage work. Only after she'd been smacked in the face with his absolute and utter betrayal did she finally leave.

Thank God Cole wasn't anything like his brother.

Was he?

With sudden clarity, she understood why she hadn't been able to tell him she loved him. She'd been waiting for the other shoe to drop, afraid the happiness they were experiencing right now wouldn't last. Would something, or someone, come between them? She'd been happy at first with Billy, had trusted him, told him every day how much she loved him. But her happiness had been short lived.

Cole was an honest man, a good man. It wasn't fair to question his fidelity, to paint him with the same brush as his cheating brother.

But no matter what she told herself, no matter how much she prayed she was wrong, her gut warned her it could happen again.

****

Lauren straddled him, her long hair falling over her face so he couldn't see her eyes. Her moist mound teased him, rubbed against him, making his body strain towards her. Sweat broke out on Cole's brow. Slowly, she lowered herself onto his erection, taking him higher and higher inside her. Her internal muscles tightened around him, his pleasure so intense it was almost painful. His focus narrowed to the joining of their bodies, and the perfect softness of her breasts in his hands.

"Yes, yes! I need you to touch me. Please, please!"

Her word was his command. He gently rolled her taut nipple between his thumb and forefinger. She responded by riding him harder, taking him deeper. He could feel his orgasm building from the soles of his feet. He couldn't wait much longer.

"Yes! Yes!"

Lauren threw back her head as she cried out her release, clasping her hands over his as they clutched her breasts. His climax came a moment later, waves rocking him over and over until he thought they might never end. But they slowed eventually, bringing him back down to earth on soft wings.

After making a quick trip to the bathroom, Lauren stretched out beside him and lay on her side. Cole placed a pillow behind her back and one between her knees to give her some support. She was getting bigger, and although she never complained, she had to be uncomfortable. He sometimes heard her leave the bed in the middle of the night, more so in the past couple of weeks, and he wondered if she couldn't sleep.

"Is that okay?"

She smiled sleepily. "Yes, it's wonderful. Thank you."

He pulled the covers over both of them and lay on

his side, looking into her face. Her eyes were closed, blue veins visible through the pale skin. She looked exhausted, as if she hadn't been sleeping properly. Yet she'd been the one to initiate sex tonight and every other night for the last two weeks. Not that he was complaining, but he was worried about her. Lately, there'd been a touch of desperation in the way she'd made love to him that scared him.

Was she already saying goodbye?

His gut clenched. He couldn't lose her, not now, not when he knew what making love with her, what *loving her* was really like. Not when it meant he'd be losing his baby daughter, too.

He reached out his hand to stroke her hair. He needed to touch her, to reassure himself she was really there in bed with him. Her eyes flickered open for a moment.

"Hmmmm. That feels good. Don't stop."

He ran his fingers through her hair, massaging her scalp. She relaxed, and soon her even breathing told him she'd fallen asleep. Slowly he lifted his hand from her hair, not wanting to wake her. He closed his eyes, trying to push away the doubts and enjoy the time he had with her.

As he started to drift off, her soft voice jolted him awake. He glanced at Lauren. Her eyes were closed tight, her breathing still the rhythmic cadence of sleep. He saw her lips move, her voice so soft he barely made out the words.

"Don't go. Please don't go."

His heart crashed against his chest. Did she mean him, or was she dreaming of Billy?

Uncertainty kept him awake most of the night.

Chapter Fifteen

March 15

Lauren stood in the middle of the baby's room and surveyed the progress. Not only had Grandma Morris used super glue in places to tack down the wallpaper, she'd pasted the last ugly layer on top of two even uglier layers. Removing it had been a huge task. For weeks she and Cole had worked together on it, with him standing on the stepladder to reach the paper near the ceiling, and Lauren working on the stuff she could more easily reach from the floor.

But it was almost done, thank God. All that was left to remove was a piece over the closet door. The problem was she couldn't reach the spot. Cole had been working on it, but he'd been called away on an emergency, and there was no telling when he'd get home. He'd specifically warned her not to climb the stepladder. She could lose her balance and fall, he'd said. She rolled her eyes at that. Her former job at the hardware store had required her to climb a ladder three times the height of this one in order to retrieve inventory in a loft storage area. She'd never once had a problem. But she'd promised Cole she'd stay off the ladder.

There was still so much to do; they had to wash the glue off the walls, paint, lay a new hardwood floor, assemble the crib, and hang the drapes. Nothing could proceed until the damn wallpaper was gone.

It was one lousy little piece of wallpaper. She could climb the ladder and strip it off the wall before Cole came home.

What he didn't see wouldn't hurt him.

She positioned the stepladder as close to the closet as she could and climbed to the top rung so she could reach to the farthest corner. But her footing was awkward in that position, so she sat on the platform at the very top of the ladder. Not only could she reach every speck of wallpaper from this vantage point, she could do it from a very stable and secure spot. She congratulated herself on her ingenuity.

She soaked the layers of wallpaper with her spray bottle, and soon, with a bit of elbow grease and her handy plastic scraper, the offending wallpaper was no more.

"One room down, the rest of the house to go."

She tried to turn her body so she could safely climb back down the ladder. But she couldn't seem to move. Her whole center of gravity had changed with her pregnancy, and she was stuck on the top of the ladder, not so much afraid to move as unable to.

Oh, great.

Brady entered the bedroom and started barking at her. "Not helpful, Brady. Unless you can suddenly use the phone to call someone to help me down, you can keep your mouth shut."

He whined, and plopped himself on the carpet in the middle of the room, looking up at her with pitiful eyes.

"Yeah, I know. Not the smartest thing I've ever

done."

There was nothing to do but to wait for Cole to come home. She only hoped he wouldn't be delayed for hours. She already had to pee.

A moment later a key rattled in the lock at the front door, and she sighed in relief. Brady perked up his ears.

"I think the cavalry's arrived, boy."

Brady ran out of the room, barking madly. A moment later he was back, with Cole right behind him. When he saw her on the top of the ladder he began to swear, his face white with fear.

"What the hell do you think you're doing up there?"

"I thought I'd bake a cake."

He clutched both her hands as he helped her slowly descend the ladder. "Very funny. Why on earth did you climb up there?"

"I've never had a problem with heights or ladders before. I didn't realize how awkward I'm getting, that's all. Once I got up there, I was stuck."

"I told you I'd scrape the damn wallpaper. Why couldn't you wait?"

"I didn't know how long you were going to be, and I want to get the job done."

He pulled her into his arms and held her tightly. "Don't ever do something like that again. If something had happened to the baby…"

"The baby's okay, Cole."

He squeezed her a little tighter. "I'll finish the work in here. I'll do anything you want. Just promise me you won't climb on that ladder again."

"I promise. I'm sorry I worried you."

"I don't know what I'd do if you lost the baby."

They both deliberately put their fears aside and talked about decorating the room. Shortly after, Cole went to the hardware store to pick up the paint in the soft yellow shade Lauren had chosen. He promised he'd have the room painted by the end of the weekend.

After he left for the store, Lauren stood in the middle of the baby's room and stared at the four bare walls, Cole's words reverberating in her head.

I don't know what I'd do if you lost the baby.

It hurt that he thought she'd take chances with their child. And maybe it was petty, but it hurt even more that he never once said he didn't know what he'd do if he lost her.

****

For the rest of the weekend, Cole worked on the baby's room. After tearing out the old, ugly carpet, he vacuumed up the dirt left behind and washed the floor. Once that was done, he gave the walls a good scrubbing to get rid of the wallpaper glue before painting the room. On Sunday afternoon, Garrett helped him install new hardwood flooring and a new light fixture. All that was left was to hang the curtains Lauren had purchased, and put together the crib.

He worked with a frenzy born of fear. He'd never been more afraid than when he'd seen Lauren perched on the top of the ladder. God only knew what kind of injury she might have sustained if she'd fallen. He couldn't get out of his head the image of her falling.

So he kept working. If the baby's room was done, she wouldn't have any excuse for making any risky climbs.

On Sunday evening, he opened the cardboard box containing the crib, removed the pieces, and laid them out on the floor. Lauren entered the room with a tray containing two mugs of tea and a plate of cookies.

"I think it's time you took a break. You've been working non-stop since Saturday morning." She set the tray on a chair and handed him a mug of tea with a splash of milk, the way he liked it. Lauren always remembered the things he liked.

"The baby will be here before we know it. I want to make sure everything's ready for her."

"It looks beautiful. I appreciate all your hard work." She sat on a chair and reached for her own tea. "There's no real hurry. We still have nearly a month until my due date. My real due date."

"Yeah, I know." Today was the sixteenth of March, one week before her supposed due date of March twenty-second. People were asking when Lauren was due. The lie tasted like acid on his tongue. It was one more deception, one more secret he had to keep.

One more hurt on his soul.

"I'm not sure what I'm going to say to people after March twenty-second passes and there's no baby."

"We'll tell them the baby's late. It's not uncommon, especially for a first child."

"But a month late? People might start getting suspicious. And what if I'm really late? What if the baby holds out until the first of May? If that happens, nobody is going to believe she's Billy's child."

Cole clamped his mouth shut to prevent the retort that wanted to spill out. *Would it be so terrible if people find out I'm Piper's father?*

Lauren turned her head and stared at a spot across the room. "I hate lying to my mother, to your mother."

Then don't! he wanted to shout. *Tell them the truth.*

Instead he said nothing. He was afraid if he asked her to tell the truth she would refuse because she was ashamed to acknowledge he was the father of her child.

He was afraid she wished Billy really was the baby's father.

****

Mia set her lunch bag on the table next to Lauren and sat down, though she hadn't been invited. "Every time I see you you're stuffing a cookie into your face. Cookies are fattening, you know."

"Really? I had no idea."

Lauren defiantly popped the rest of her cookie into her mouth. Damn if she'd allow Mia to get to her.

But it was hard. The closer Lauren got to her due date, the more Mia seemed to enjoy undermining her confidence. Even though she did her best to avoid her, Mia went out of her way to seek her out, cornering her any time she was alone and speaking aloud all the worries and fears she tried to keep hidden.

She pushed herself to her feet and started gathering the remnants of her lunch. She should have brought the Civic today. Her mother had lent it to her for the duration of her pregnancy, and beyond, until she could buy a car for herself, she'd said. She could have gone home for lunch the way she had for the last couple of weeks. But it had been snowing this morning, and Cole had insisted on driving her. Since he often saw clients over the noon hour, she'd had to bring her lunch, even though she'd known it meant another confrontation with Mia was inevitable. She hadn't told Cole about her harassment. If she did, it would mean bringing out into the open her deepest fears about their future.

"Running away?"

"You're not exactly my favorite lunch companion."

Mia laughed. "I'll give you credit, Lauren. You're good with the snappy comebacks. Your smart mouth may intrigue Cole enough to keep you around. But I doubt it."

Lauren threw her plastic containers of half-eaten food into her bag, her appetite gone. "Are you always this much of a bitch, or are you saving it all for me?"

Mia ignored her dig. "Surely you're not so dense that you don't realize Cole simply feels sorry for you and responsible for his brother's widow and unborn child. He's got some kind of hero complex. But don't fool yourself into thinking he loves you. One day soon he'll come to his senses and realize what a leech you are, the same way Billy did."

"Goodbye, Mia." She headed for the break room door, praying she couldn't see how much her last remark had hurt.

"Run, Lauren, run!" Mia's derisive laughter followed her out of the room. She approached her desk at the reception area, where Audrey was covering the phones for her. Audrey looked up at her in surprise.

"You're back already? You've only been gone ten minutes."

"I'm ready to go back to work."

Audrey glanced toward the break room door. "Did Mia say something to you? Is that why you're upset?"

"I'm not upset." She hoped Audrey wouldn't see through her lie. But her friend was far more perceptive than she gave her credit for.

"Yes, you are, and it's not good for you or the baby. Why don't you tell Dr. Waverly what she's doing? Maybe he'd do something about her."

"I don't want to drag Dr. Waverly into this."

"What about Cole? What does he say about Mia harassing you?"

Lauren looked away, embarrassed. "Nothing."

"Nothing? I can't believe Cole wouldn't stick up for you." Audrey grabbed her hand. "You have told him, haven't you?"

"I don't want to upset him."

More lies. She was afraid to tell him the truth. About a lot of things.

Audrey stood. "I'm going to go in there and give her a piece of my mind."

"No, please, don't do that. I'll handle it. I promise."

"Lauren, I don't understand. Why are you letting Mia get away with bullying you? Why won't you allow anyone to help?"

Because I'm afraid Mia is right. I'm afraid Cole will soon discover feeling sorry for me isn't enough to sustain our marriage. I'm afraid my biggest fear is true—that Cole insisted on marrying me only because of his sense of responsibility for the baby. That he had no choice but to marry me.

She choked back her tears, her composure hanging by a thread. She didn't want to lose it at work and give Mia even more ammunition.

"Please don't say anything," she pleaded. "I'm begging you."

"Okay, okay. If that's what you want. But I'm going to make sure Mia doesn't take her lunch break at the same time as you from now on. Will you at least let me do that much?"

Lauren nodded, relief making her knees weak. She

sank into her chair. Audrey put her arm around her shoulders.

"If you change your mind, or you want to talk, I hope you know that I'm here to listen, okay?"

Lauren swallowed her tears once more. "That means a lot to me. Thank you."

With one last squeeze to her shoulder, Audrey left the reception area. Lauren closed her eyes and concentrated on taking deep breaths to calm herself and the baby, who kicked madly against her ribs, obviously picking up on her distress. For her sake, she had to keep calm.

And for her sake, she had to keep her family together.

****

Lauren barely said a word to Cole on the drive home. She didn't mean to give him the silent treatment, but she didn't know what to say. She'd teetered on the edge of tears all afternoon, ever since her confrontation with Mia. She was afraid if she started to talk, the tears would follow. She stared out the side window and watched the snow falling to the ground.

"You're very quiet. Are you okay?"

Lauren glanced at Cole. His worried expression caused guilt to roil in her stomach. The last thing she wanted was to upset him. She made herself smile.

"I'm fine. A little tired, that's all."

He reached across the bench seat of the truck to take her hand. "It's only five more weeks until your due date. I know you wanted to work right up until the baby came, but maybe you should cut back your hours, or even better, stay at home and rest."

"There's no need. I'm fine, really."

"If it's about the money, I don't want you to worry. I'll make sure you have everything you and the baby need."

She squeezed his hand, loving him for his generosity. "I know you will, but really, I feel fine, and there's no reason I can't work a little longer. It's not like I'm on my feet all day or doing something physically exerting."

"Maybe not, but any kind of work can be stressful. I don't want you to take any chances."

"I won't, Cole. I promise."

He nodded and turned his attention back to the road. "Good. As soon as we get home I want you to lie down for a while and rest while I make supper. Okay?"

"Okay."

She relaxed against the headrest and stared at his profile as he drove. He took such good care of her. Surely, that was a kind of love.

But she didn't really know. She was carrying his child, and Lauren knew Cole loved the baby and would do anything to protect her.

Perhaps that was all they had.

True to his word, Cole helped her take off her parka and snow boots at the front door and then steered her to their bedroom, where he instructed her to lie down on the bed. After covering her with an extra blanket, he kissed her forehead.

"Sleep well, sweetheart."

Lauren grabbed the front of his sweatshirt and pulled him closer. "Why don't you stay with me? I can think of something better to do than sleep."

He kissed her forehead once more. "You're tired. You're supposed to be resting."

“I’ve made a miraculous recovery.” She grinned to hide her desperation, her fear.

“Don’t tempt me.” He tried to look stern, but his smile gave him away.

She kissed his jawline. “But I like tempting you. It’s so much fun.”

“How am I supposed to look after you if you don’t cooperate?”

“The best way you can look after me is by making love to me.”

She slid her hand down his body to his crotch and silently rejoiced when her hand met the hard length of his erection through his jeans.

“You can’t deny you want me.”

He caught her hand, stilling her questing fingers. “I always want you.”

The teasing was gone from his eyes, replaced by an intensity she’d never seen before. It humbled her to know he still desired her this much, even in the latter stages of her pregnancy. She wanted to show him how much she loved him, even though she couldn’t put her feelings into words.

“I want you, too. Stay, Cole. Please. I need you.”

“I’ll never walk away from you. Not if you need me.”

He kissed her, ravaging her mouth until she was shaking with need. He quickly undressed her, then stripped off his own clothes. Pushing her back against the pillows, he parted her legs and kissed his way up her thighs. Lauren’s body trembled in anticipation. At the first stroke of his tongue, she came undone. Her body bucked and shook with delicious tremors, but Cole stayed with her, licking and sucking until she felt another orgasm building. Once more it exploded inside her. Tiny pinpricks of light flashed behind her closed eyelids like a miniature fireworks display.

Feeling utterly boneless, she collapsed against the pillows. As Cole lay down beside her, she snuggled against him.

"I believe it's your turn."

"It is." A tremor rippled through his body at her touch. "I want to try something new."

Excitement built inside her once more. She couldn't believe it. She'd already had two orgasms. But Cole had the power to bring her to climax with a simple word.

He helped her off the bed and led her to a small chair in a corner of the room. He sat on the chair, his penis proudly erect.

"If you sit on my lap, we won't put so much pressure on your stomach. And you can control how deep you want me inside you."

She leaned over him to whisper in his ear.

"I want you deep."

"So do I, baby. But I only want you to go as deep as feels good. Okay?"

"Okay." She loved him for thinking of her comfort over his pleasure.

But more than anything, she wanted to please him. *Needed* to please him.

Maybe then he'd stay.

Bracing her hands on his shoulders, she straddled the chair, then carefully lowered herself over him. Her breath caught. At this angle, Cole's arousal pressed against sensitive nerve endings inside her she'd never known existed before. The sensation was exquisitely erotic. She could feel herself on the brink of another climax.

But this was about Cole and his pleasure.

She slid down his shaft until he was fully buried inside her, taking a moment to savor the feel of him. Then she lifted her hips, sliding slowly up his length. Cole made an inarticulate sound in his throat, his eyes glazed with passion. She impaled herself again, slid over him again and again, knowing both of them were on the brink. When Cole took her breast in his mouth, suckling on the hard tip, she was lost. A moment later he cried out her name as he spilled into her.

For a long time they held each other, trying to catch their breaths. Lauren couldn't bear for this perfect moment to end. She wanted to stay like this, with their bodies joined, forever. She'd never experienced this closeness, heart and soul, with anyone before. She'd never loved anyone the way she loved Cole.

She and Billy had been a mistake. She understood that now. She was in love with Cole, and he was the best man she knew.

Fear made her shiver, despite the sweat that slicked her body. She held him a little tighter and prayed they would always be together.

Chapter Sixteen

March 30

The labor rooms in the Bismarck Hospital looked a lot like ordinary bedrooms. Soft lighting and the blue color of the walls gave the rooms a soothing aura. Care had been taken to make the rooms a little less clinical than the rest of the hospital. Lauren had read that the place where a woman gave birth should be similar to the place where she conceived. She'd chuckled reading that. It would be tough to recreate a room in the hospital that mimicked the spot in the pasture where she got pregnant. The hospital likely had rules about campfires and beds of grass.

She held Cole's hand as they toured the facility. There were three birthing rooms, but they could only see two of them since one was currently in use.

The instructor pointed out the large tub. "Our rooms are equipped with baths. Many of our mothers find a bath or shower to be very soothing during labor. Our goal here is to provide a calming environment for our mothers to give birth, and to give women and their partners whatever they need to have a natural, safe birth. We want every mother to have a good experience here."

"What if something goes wrong?" one of the mothers asked. "What if there are complications?"

"If that happens, you're right next door to the facilities and staff of the hospital. You don't have to worry about being far from help."

Though the rooms were nice and every effort had been made to create a homey feel that was completely safe, she couldn't stop worrying. She could handle the pain of labor and delivery, as scary as that sounded. But she was terrified something could happen to the baby.

What if something went wrong during delivery?

What if her baby didn't make it?

She shivered at the thought.

Cole squeezed her hand.

"Are you okay?" he whispered.

"Yes, of course." She was being ridiculous. Dr. McKenzie had assured her on numerous occasions that everything was proceeding normally. There was nothing to worry about. There was no point making Cole anxious as well.

The tour was soon over, and they left for home. When they stopped at a red light, Cole reached across the seat and seized her hand.

"You're very quiet."

"It was a lot to take in tonight."

"Are you scared? Because it's okay to be scared."

"Is it?"

"Sure." Releasing her hand, he signaled for a right turn and headed east on Interstate 94. "There wasn't a mother there tonight who wasn't at least a little nervous. Your body is going to go through an enormous ordeal—a very natural one, but a big one none the less. It's understandable you should feel apprehensive."

She decided to trust him with her fears. "What scares me most is something going wrong during the birth, or something being wrong with the baby. I know it's stupid, but I can't stop thinking about it."

As they left the city, he reached for her hand once more. "I know I can't make you any promises, but I feel like this baby was meant to be. She's going to be born healthy and whole. Everything's going to be okay."

Lauren entwined her fingers with his. As long as Cole was beside her, she'd be fine. He was the voice of reason to counteract her wild imaginings. He was her rock. Her everything.

"It's cold tonight. I think it's a good night to cuddle in front of the fire."

He grinned. "Sounds good. I'll make hot chocolate. I even bought mini-marshmallows."

"You're my hero."

He squeezed her hand. "Don't ever forget it, baby."

****

Cole sat in the Homestead Restaurant having a cup of coffee with Dr. Waverly. It was Saturday morning, and they'd performed an emergency caesarian section on a cow a short time ago. Doing surgery in a cow barn was never his first choice, since there was always increased risk of infection, but the barn had been clean, if not sterile, and mother and calf seemed to be doing well. Cole lifted his cup and saluted the older vet.

"I'm glad you were available this morning. It's always good to have an extra set of hands."

"My pleasure," Dr. Waverly said. "It's good to know my skills haven't completely atrophied."

"No chance of that."

"I'm quite happy to let younger vets like you and Jamie take over the midnight calls and the emergencies. Lord knows I did my share of those. But I like to keep my hand in once in a while. Keeps the blood pumping."

"Yeah, it does." He had to admit that it was the toughest cases that kept veterinary medicine exciting for him. Every case was different and rewarding, but it was the most difficult ones that challenged him and kept him striving to be the best vet he could be.

"How's Lauren doing? I can't believe she's working so late into her pregnancy. Isn't she due any day now?"

He'd been asked that question repeatedly in the last week, by friends, people he met on the street, even his mother. Everyone believed her due date had passed, rather than being three weeks away. He skirted around the question.

"Lauren's doing fine. She's determined to work until she goes into labor."

"She's an amazing girl. When's her due date again?"

"It was March twenty-second, but you know how first pregnancies are. The baby is taking her time." He hated having to lie, especially to Dr. Waverly. He was a good person and a good boss to both him and Lauren. He didn't deserve to be deceived.

"I know what you're going through. Our first child was born nearly two weeks later than her original due date. My wife was pretty uncomfortable by the end. Tell Lauren she doesn't need to work to the last minute if she doesn't feel up to it." Dr. Waverly drained his coffee cup. "I should get going. My wife wants to make a trip to Bismarck to do some shopping today. Unless something happens with Lauren, I'll see you at the clinic on Monday morning."

"Goodbye. And thanks again."

With a wave, he left the diner. Cole was also ready to leave. With Lauren so close to her due date, he didn't like to be away from her for any length of time. He finished his coffee and left some money on the table before getting to his feet.

"Hey, Cole! How are you?"

Sam Miller walked toward him, his hand outstretched. Though Cole liked him well enough, he'd been Billy's friend back in high school rather than his. Sam had always been in awe of Billy, which was likely why his brother allowed him to hang around.

He shook Sam's hand. "I'm well. I thought you were working out of state."

"I was, but I'm home for a few months. I heard you and Lauren are married now. Congratulations."

Cole watched his face carefully for any sign of disapproval to his marriage. He didn't give a damn what Sam thought of him, but he wouldn't tolerate any disparaging remarks against Lauren.

"Thank you."

"How is she? I heard she's having a baby. Has she given birth yet?"

"She's very well. The baby will arrive…soon."

"I'm glad she's doing so well. I'm sure Billy would be grateful to you for taking care of her and his child."

Cole wanted to smash his fist through Sam's earnest face. He wanted to yell at him that Lauren was his wife now, not Billy's, and the child she was carrying was *his* flesh and blood. Instead, he nodded and smiled, then quickly left the diner before he said or did something he'd regret.

It wasn't the first time his daughter had been referred to as Billy's baby. His mother did it all the time. She was always quick to remind him that if Billy were alive, Lauren would still be happily married to him.

He was thoroughly sick of being thought of as her second choice, someone she'd turned to because she'd been desperate. And it killed him that everyone in town believed his baby girl belonged to Billy. Sometimes he thought about moving away from Masonville once the baby was born, somewhere far away where no one knew their history. Some place where the three of them could simply be a family and not have to pretend.

Though he'd never brought up the idea of relocating, he didn't think Lauren would want to move away from her family, especially now that she was having a baby. And he had his mother to look after. He was her only family now.

How long was he supposed to pretend Piper didn't belong to him? Until she was in school? Until she left home?

He hopped into his truck and slammed the door shut. For a moment, he stared out the windshield at the snow-covered streets of his hometown and wished things could be different. Wished *he* could be different. A different man would demand to be recognized as the father of his child. He wouldn't be afraid to learn the truth of his wife's feelings toward him. He would tell his wife that he loved her more than anything in the world.

But he wasn't a different man. With a sigh, he put the key in the ignition and started the truck.

****

On Monday afternoon, Lauren looked into the washroom mirror at work and frowned at her reflection.

Dark circles under her eyes made her look like a tired raccoon.

A very pregnant tired raccoon.

At thirty-eight weeks pregnant, it was getting difficult to sit for long periods of time at her desk. Sometimes Lauren used the headphones to answer the phone while standing, but she found that her lower back ached if she stood too long, especially if she had to bend over to use the keyboard on her computer. So she'd sit for a while, until that became too uncomfortable again. With all the ups and downs, she was starting to feel like a pop-up toaster.

Today was especially bad. Her back ached whether she stood or sat. The baby had shifted so that she was lying low, directly over Lauren's bladder. Every move, every kick sent Lauren to the bathroom. She'd barely slept the night before.

Maybe Cole was right about staying home until the baby came. It wasn't like she was terribly productive at work right now. She was too tired from lack of sleep to be effective. Her temporary replacement had already been trained and was ready to fill in for her for a few weeks. Maybe now was the time. She'd talk to Cole as soon as he got back from his call.

As she turned the corner to head back to the reception desk, she saw Mia rifling through her desk.

"What are you doing?"

Mia slammed a drawer shut. "Nothing. I was looking for a pen."

"A pen? There are at least three pens sitting on the top of my desk. Try again, Mia. What were you doing in my desk?"

"I don't have anything to say to you. I'm going

back to work."

She brushed past Lauren and hurried to the back of the clinic. Lauren checked her desk. The cash drawer was unlocked, and a quick count showed about a hundred dollars was missing. Anger sizzled through her.

Enough.

She marched to the back room. Mia sat on a stool peering into a microscope.

"Give it back," Lauren demanded, holding out her hand. "Give back the money you stole from the cash box right now and maybe I won't phone the police."

"I don't know what you're talking about."

"I'm talking about you being a thief."

Mia turned away. "You're crazy."

"Fine. I'll get Dr. Waverly. He can throw you out on your ass while I call the police."

She turned to leave, but Mia grabbed her arm, stopping her. Her fingernails dug into her skin.

"Let go of me."

"Dr. Waverly gave me his key."

Lauren stared at her in surprise. "Why would he do that?"

"Because I told him I needed some supplies."

"That doesn't wash, Mia. If you really needed supplies for work, all you had to do was ask me to get it for you. I order everything the clinic uses. But we can clear this up in about thirty seconds. I'll ask Dr. Waverly if he really gave you the key to the cash drawer."

"That's what you want, isn't it? To get rid of me. But I'm not going anywhere. If you say one word to Dr. Waverly, I'm going to tell him that you've been harassing me since the day you started working here. Who do you think he's going to fire?"

"You're the one who's crazy. Nobody here will believe I've been harassing you. Everybody knows what a conniving bitch you are."

"Oh, right. Everyone knows how perfect you are. Sweet little Lauren. Billy and I used to laugh at how gullible you were."

"Not so gullible. I knew Billy cheated on me. Did you know about all his other women? The ones who hung around the hockey rink for a chance to sleep with the players? Believe me, Billy took full advantage of every opportunity he was given."

Mia's face changed, and she dug her nails deeper into Lauren's skin. "You're lying. Billy loved me."

Lauren tugged on her arm. "Maybe he did, but that didn't stop him from screwing everything he could get his hands on. Did you know he didn't die alone on that Georgia highway? The police told me there was a woman in the car with him. She must have been new, because I didn't recognize her name."

"No! He loved me! If it hadn't been for you, he would have married me."

"Did he tell you he couldn't marry you because I wouldn't give him a divorce? I provided a very convenient excuse, but the truth was he never once asked me for a divorce."

"You bitch," Mia spat. "Everything goes your way, doesn't it? You think you know everything. Did you know I was sleeping with Cole?"

Spots danced in front of Lauren's eyes, and for a moment she thought she'd faint. She steadied herself by hanging onto the back of a chair. "You're lying. Cole wouldn't cheat on me."

Mia laughed, the sound ugly and bitter. "Oh, wouldn't he? He's pretty good, not as good as Billy, of course, but he services me very well."

"That's a damn lie!" She wrenched her arm away from Mia.

"He's got this cute little birthmark on his left hip. It looks like a map of Italy. I tease him about it all the time."

Lauren covered her mouth with her hand. A voice screamed in her head, *No, no, no! Not again. Dear God, not again!*

She stumbled out of the lab, Mia's laughter ringing in her ears. A few steps outside the lab she ran into Audrey. The older woman grabbed her shoulders and peered into her face.

"Lauren, what's wrong? What happened?"

"I'm not feeling well. I need to go home."

"I'll drive you."

"No! I have my car here today. I can drive myself home. Please tell Dr. Waverly I had to leave."

"Maybe we should take you straight to the hospital. I'll call Cole—"

"No! I'm fine. I only need to lie down for a while."

"Lauren, you shouldn't be alone. Maybe you're in labor."

"No, I'm sure I'm not. I'm fine, just tired. I need to lie down. Please, I have to go."

Reluctantly Audrey stepped back. "Okay, honey. But if you need me, you call me right away. Okay?"

She nodded, unable to speak. Audrey helped her put on her coat and boots and walked her to her car. She opened the car door and helped Lauren slide into the driver's seat.

"You're sure this is what you want to do? I could come with you."

"You have to work, Audrey. Please tell Dr. Waverly, okay?"

Audrey nodded, though she still looked worried. "I will."

She closed the door, and Lauren drove home slowly, trying to stay focused on the snow-covered road instead of on the bomb Mia had dropped on her life. The only way she could know about the birthmark on Cole's hip was if she'd slept with him.

She managed to keep it together until she got home. Was this really her home anymore? She'd thought this house could be a refuge for their family. She'd thought she belonged here. But now everything was messed up.

Gone.

Lauren curled up on the sofa as tears flooded her eyes.

Everything was gone.

****

Cole pulled his truck into the driveway behind Lauren's car. After receiving Audrey's worried phone call, he wrapped up his examination of the cow that he and Dr. Waverly had performed the C-section on a couple of days ago and drove as fast as he could back to town. Was Lauren in labor? If she was, why hadn't she called him?

The house was totally dark, further worrying him. He unlocked the front door and stepped inside. The house was cold, empty. Had her parents taken her to the hospital? Again, he wondered why she hadn't called him.

"Lauren? Lauren, are you here?"

No answer. He pulled off his boots and turned on the lights as he stepped into the living room. He found her on the sofa, curled in a fetal position. Her eyes were open, staring straight ahead. Relief mixed with dread. He sat next to her on the sofa and laid his hand on her hip.

"Lauren, baby, are you all right? Why were you lying here in the dark?"

"I've been afraid all along that you only married me because I was pregnant, and now I know for sure."

Fear formed a painful knot in his stomach. "What are you talking about?"

"She told me. Mia told me you slept with her."

He closed his eyes. He should have known that Mia would torment Lauren, that she'd try to drive a wedge between them.

"It happened a long time ago, before you came back to Masonville."

"That's not what Mia says. She says you're still sleeping with her."

"That's a lie!"

"Why should I believe you? Billy lied to me. He lied to me all through our marriage. I thought you were different, but now I find you had something in common. You both slept with Mia."

"I'm not anything like Billy! I slept with Mia twice, months before you came home, and I ended it back then. It was a mistake from the beginning."

She pushed herself to a sitting position, and he saw the tracks of dried tears on her cheeks and the pain in her eyes.

"How can I believe you?" Her face contorted in anguish as fresh tears filled her eyes. "Did the two of you laugh at me while you were in bed together?"

He grabbed her shoulders, desperation clawing at his gut. "No! I told you, I haven't been with Mia for months. I only want you!"

She shook her head, tears streaking down her face. "I trusted you. I fell in love with you. You *made* me fall in love with you. I thought I meant something to you."

"You mean everything to me. I love you."

She shook her head. "You don't love me, not really. I'm nothing more than a responsibility to you."

"Don't tell me how I feel." Desperation turned to anger in a flash. Cole jumped to his feet and began to pace. "I've been in love with you since I was sixteen years old, but you never saw me, not really. You only had eyes for Billy. It nearly killed me when you married him, but I stuffed down my anger and hurt and congratulated both of you, because really, what else could I do?"

"No, that can't be true."

"It's true, all right. I wish to God it wasn't. I tried to push away my feelings for you, tried to love other women, but none of them were you. None of them compared to you. I thought I'd get over you, but I never did."

Her eyes were wide with shock. "Cole—"

"Billy guessed the truth. I found out he'd been cheating on you, and I confronted him. We had a huge fight, beat each other till we were both bloody. He told me I was jealous because you'd rejected me. He said you'd never want me, that you'd always be tied to him, no matter what happened. And he was right." He gave a bark of mirthless laughter. “He’s dead and he still comes between us.”

“That’s not true!”

“Isn’t it? You’re the one who’s still hung up on a man who used you and cheated on you. Do you know how it makes me feel to have everyone believe Billy is my child’s father? Are you ever going to tell your family I’m the baby’s father? Will you ever tell our daughter the truth?”

Lauren closed her eyes, her head in her hands. “Please, Cole, stop.”

“At first I thought you were embarrassed by the timing of your pregnancy and that was why you wanted people to believe the baby was Billy’s. But that’s not the truth at all. You wish the baby was his. You’re not over him. You’ll never be over him.”

“Cole, no! Please, don’t do this!”

He couldn’t listen to her cry for his brother. He had to get away. Pushing his feet into his boots, he grabbed his jacket and ran to his truck. With a squeal of tires, he pulled out of the driveway.

Chapter Seventeen

March 30

For the next couple of hours, Cole drove aimlessly, trying to get his emotions under control. The more clear-headed he become the angrier he was at himself. He'd lost control, yelled at Lauren. He'd said things to her he'd never meant to say, things better left unsaid. She'd never forgive him for what he'd said.

Was their marriage over?

The thought made him sick to his stomach. He stopped the truck at the side of the road, realizing with a start he was near the spot where he'd met Lauren on the day of Billy's funeral, the place he'd made love to her for the first time. Their special place, she'd called it.

He got out of the truck and walked through the deep snow, crawled between the lengths of barbed wire, and made it to the clearing in the trees. Though it was only about six in the evening, darkness closed in around him. The only light came from the full moon peeking over the top of the trees.

As he stood in the clearing, memories swamped him. He and Billy and Lauren as teenagers, laughing, teasing each other, smoking cigarettes and drinking beer. Through the years, they'd loved each other and sometimes hated each other. The three of them would always be connected, even in death.

He wouldn't blame Lauren if she never forgave him. He could only pray she would.

There was only one thing he knew for certain. Mia would never hurt her again. Pulling out his cell phone, he punched in Dr. Waverly's number.

"Hello?"

"Tom, it's Cole. Something's come up, and I need to talk to you. Can I come to your house? I can be there in about fifteen minutes."

"Yes, of course. I'll be waiting for you."

He ended the call and put the phone back in his pocket. With one last look around the clearing, he retraced his steps to his truck, renewed purpose in his stride.

He wouldn't let anyone hurt Lauren again. Especially him.

****

Lauren heard the front door open sometime past midnight and nearly cried with relief. Cole had been gone for hours, and she'd been sick with worry. He'd been so angry at her. What if that anger had caused him to have a terrible accident?

Or maybe he'd decided not to come home again.

She slipped out of bed and stood at the closed door of the master bedroom, waiting. She heard his footsteps in the hallway. Would he come to her? She laid her hand on the knob, wanting to open the door but afraid to make that leap of faith.

The footsteps stopped. For a few seconds there was silence, and she held her breath. A moment later she heard him walk away. The soft click of the guest bedroom door echoed in her ears like a gunshot. For long seconds, she debated whether to go to him, to apologize. If she went to him, would he forgive her? Or would he tell her to leave the room, and leave his life?

Her fingers tightened on the knob for a moment before letting go. After the fight they'd had, she was too much of a coward to find out.

She returned to the bed, stepping carefully to avoid the creaky floorboards that would alert Cole she was awake. She crawled beneath the blankets, and covered her mouth with her hand to muffle her sobs.

She'd hurt Cole in so many ways. Why had she believed Mia's story? Cole had always been her friend, had always told her the truth.

Maybe he hadn't always told her the truth. All these years and he'd never told her until tonight that he'd loved her for so long.

Would it have made a difference if he'd told her back when they were kids? Probably not. She'd been so infatuated with Billy she couldn't see anything or anyone else. If she'd known Cole loved her, they likely couldn't have stayed friends through all the intervening years.

Cole hadn't told her he'd known about Billy's infidelity, either. If he'd told her he'd been cheating on her before she had a chance to find out for herself, she wouldn't have believed him. It would have destroyed their friendship.

But whatever Cole had done or didn't do, her sins were far greater. She'd allowed everyone to believe Billy had fathered her baby. It had been the easy thing to do, the thing that permitted her to keep her pride. But her pride meant nothing now. She hadn't thought how Cole would feel to be denied his rightful place in his daughter's life. She'd hurt him so badly. No wonder he'd lashed out at her.

She'd been such a stupid fool. How could Cole ever forgive her?

Sobs wracked her body. She was sick to her stomach, and her back ached, but she couldn't stop crying.

She loved Cole. If she lost him she had no one to blame but herself.

****

Cole woke early the next morning after a fitful sleep. After speaking to Dr. Waverly at his house, he'd driven around until midnight, too unsure of his welcome at home to make an appearance. But worry brought him home. Lauren was too close to her due date to leave her alone for too long.

He'd arrived home to find their bedroom door closed, a sure signal she didn't want him near her. So he spent the night in the guest room, tossing and turning.

All was quiet as he emerged from the bathroom after a quick shower. He stood in front of the master bedroom door, his heart racing. He had to make sure she was okay. Silently, he turned the knob and opened the door. Lauren lay on her side, one hand over her pregnant belly, her hair spread wildly over the white pillow. Sheets and blankets were twisted as if she'd done a lot of tossing and turning herself. The dog, sprawled beside her, lifted his head and gave a desultory wag of his tail before going back to sleep.

His gut twisted. She may never want him in her bed again. And there was a strong likelihood that after what he'd said to her she wouldn't want him in her life anymore either.

Quietly, he closed the door and left the house.

As soon as he got to work, he and Tom called Mia to his office. After shutting the door, Dr. Waverly turned to Mia.

"Some very disturbing news has come to my attention regarding your behavior. We're dismissing you. We no longer want you working in this clinic."

Mia blinked in surprise. "You're firing me? Are you kidding? Three years ago, you begged me to come work for you."

"That was before I got to know you. I've had several complaints about you from your co-workers over the years, and now Cole has told me about the altercation you had with Lauren."

"She's lying!" Mia hissed. "She's the one who stole the money from the cash drawer, not me. She's trying to pin it on me because she's jealous."

Cole glanced at Tom Waverly in surprise. Stolen money? What the hell was she talking about? Tom kept his gaze focused on Mia.

"Actually, neither Lauren nor Cole said anything about you stealing money from the cash drawer, but that gives me one more reason to get rid of you. I want you to gather your things. Cole and I will escort you off the property in five minutes."

"You can't do this!" She turned to Cole. "Tell him! Tell him you need me here."

"The only thing I'm going to say to you is that if you ever contact my wife again, I'll have the police charge you with harassment."

Mia's face twisted with rage. "Perfect little Lauren. You think the little bitch can do no wrong. She's nothing but a faker, a manipulator. Billy told me all about her."

Cole's rage turned cold. He grasped the armrests of Mia's chair and snarled into her face.

"Don't ever talk to me about my wife or my brother. Once you leave here, I never want to see your face again."

Five minutes later he and Dr. Waverly escorted an angry Mia to her car. She slammed her door and peeled out of the parking lot, her tires spitting snow and gravel in every direction. Cole sighed in relief.

"Well, that's done," Dr. Waverly said. "I guess we'll be looking for a new technician."

"Next time let's be more careful about who we hire, and get character references as well as work references."

"Amen to that. Lauren told me money had been going missing, but I refused to believe anyone on staff was responsible. If I'd paid more attention to her concerns, maybe we could have avoided this whole ugly scene."

"I doubt it. I think Mia was trying to discredit her, maybe get her fired."

"How is Lauren?"

Cole didn't know how to answer that. "She's at home. I'd like her to stay there and rest until the baby comes. She shouldn't be under a lot of stress right now."

"Maybe you should go home, too, so you can be with her. We can reschedule some of your appointments. I can take care of the most urgent ones."

"We don't need to do that. I can get to her in minutes if she goes into labor." Would Lauren even want him in the house after the things he'd said?

"All right, but I think we should limit your appointments to in-clinic until the baby comes, in case you have to make a fast trip to the hospital. If there's some kind of emergency that requires a farm call, I'll take it."

Cole nodded. He wondered if Lauren would still allow him to be present at the birth of their daughter. The thought of not being there, of not being part of their lives, caused an ache in his chest.

Dr. Waverly clapped him on the back. "Come on inside. It's cold out here."

He followed him into the building, his thoughts racing. Lauren was all he'd ever wanted. His jealousy and insecurity had ruined the best thing that ever happened to him.

****

Lauren woke past noon to a pounding head and pain in her lower back. The events of the previous night rushed back, swamping her with guilt and fear. Somehow she had to make things right. But how?

She carefully pushed herself to a sitting position and swung her legs to the side of the bed. Her headache intensified at the movement, and she stopped to take a few deep breaths, her head in her hands. Finally, the pounding subsided enough to allow her to get to her feet and grab her robe. Brady jumped off the bed and followed her to the kitchen. She opened the back door so he could go outside to do his business, and after he returned, she scooped kibble into his bowl. He wolfed it down in a few bites, then looked hopefully at her, as if expecting more.

"That's all you get. Cole doesn't want you to get too fat."

At the mention of Cole's name, his ears perked up. Lauren scratched his head.

"You love him too, don't you."

The tears started again. She'd thought she'd cried them all out the night before, but still they kept coming. She had to prove to Cole that she loved him. Somehow, she had to find a way to make things right between them.

She felt cramping in her lower abdomen. *Oh, God!* Did this mean she was in the early stages of labor?

Splaying her hands across her belly, she whispered, "You have to wait, Piper. I have to make things right with your daddy before you're born. I want him to be the first person to see you."

Her way forward suddenly became clear, and she saw what she needed to do. It was going to be difficult, probably the hardest thing she'd ever done, but nothing was going to stop her from fighting for her family.

****

Tom Waverly held the x-ray up to the light box. "What do you think?"

Cole carefully examined the dark mass over the dog's left kidney. "I think it's a tumor. Hard to say whether it's malignant until we remove it. From the size of it, we'll likely have to take the kidney as well. I don't believe there's any other option at this point."

"That was my thinking as well. Thanks for confirming." Tom sighed. "The dog is nearly ten years old. I don't know whether the owners can afford an expensive surgery like this. They might opt to simply euthanize."

Cole nodded. The reality of his profession was that every animal couldn't be saved. Sometimes the costs were simply too high. The best they could do at times was to make the animal comfortable and ensure it didn't suffer.

His phone rang, breaking off his thoughts. As he pulled his cell from his pocket and saw his home number on the screen, his heart lifted.

"Excuse me. I have to take this."

Dr. Waverly nodded, and Cole left the room, pressing the talk button as he closed the door.

"Lauren?"

"Hi."

"Are you okay?"

"I'm fine."

"That's good."

He closed his eyes, nearly groaning at this utterly inane conversation. There was so much more he wanted to say to her, starting with *I love you.* But the words stuck in his throat.

"We need to talk. Will you be…will you be coming home after work?"

She sounded tired, her voice a little shaky.

"Yes, if you want me to, I'll be there."

She cleared her throat. "I want you to. Like I said, we need to talk. There's a lot of things we've left unsaid, a lot of things we need to get out in the open."

His stomach swooped at her words. He pressed his fingers against his closed eyelids, afraid of what she wanted to tell him.

"I'll be there about four-thirty."

"Thank you. Goodbye."

"Bye."

He hit the Off button and stuck the phone in his pocket once more. Whatever Lauren wanted to say to him, he had no choice but to listen.

He prayed she didn't want to say goodbye.

****

Cole pulled his truck into the driveway a couple of hours later and was surprised to see Garrett's truck there. Lauren's parents' car and her sister Charlotte's Jeep sat on the street in front of the house.

Why was everyone here? Her call had given him hope they could work things out, alone. Had she asked her family over for moral support so she could tell him goodbye?

Another thought hit him. Were they here because she'd gone into labor? Was she all right?

He raced into the house and threw open the door. Lauren sat in the recliner with her feet up, her mother and sister standing behind her. Garrett and Robert Saunders stood next to the fireplace, and he was surprised to see his mother there as well. What the hell was going on?

He went to Lauren, not bothering to take off his wet shoes. Kneeling by her chair, he reached for her hand.

"Are you okay?"

She squeezed his hand, her face tense. "I will be."

"What's going on?"

She put her feet on the floor. "Can you help me up? Now that you're here, there's something I need to say to everyone."

Cole put his arm around her waist and gently helped her stand. She didn't look well. Lines of fatigue marred her pale face. The stress of the last couple of days showed in her haunted eyes. He saw pain in her eyes as well.

"I'm going to call Dr. McKenzie," he said.

She held his arm with surprising strength, stopping him from reaching for his phone. "No. I have something to say first. To everyone."

A shiver raced through her body, and he held her a little tighter. She gave him a grateful smile.

"It's long past time that everyone I love and care about knows the truth. The baby I'm carrying is Cole's child, not Billy's."

He heard his mother's gasp. "No!"

Lauren trembled, but her eyes were dry, her expression determined. "We didn't plan it. We turned to each other in mutual need and found something wonderful. I didn't tell anyone the truth because I was afraid of what you and everyone else in Masonville would think of me for getting pregnant on the day of Billy's funeral." She turned to look into Cole's face. "But now I only care what my husband thinks of me. He's the most important person in the world to me, and I love him."

Cole's throat closed with emotion. The courage it must have taken for her to speak out like this was beyond his comprehension. He'd never been prouder of her. And he'd never loved her more.

"How do you know for sure?" his mother said, a tremor in her voice. "How can you be so certain the baby isn't Billy's?"

Lauren closed her eyes and inhaled before answering the question, as if gathering her courage once more. "Because we hadn't slept together for some time before his death, and because, just before his accident, Billy told me he'd had a vasectomy right after my second miscarriage."

"No! My son wouldn't do that!"

"I'm sorry, Ella, but it's the truth. We had a big fight. Billy got news that he was being traded again. I said I was tired of moving around and changing jobs. I told him that maybe it was a sign he should give up hockey and we should move home. We could start all over again, have the family we always wanted.

"Billy was so angry. He said I'd never believed in his dream, I'd never supported him. He'd never move back to a hick town like Masonville, and he had no interest in having a family. He said…" She paused to inhale, and slowly exhale. "He said he was glad I'd miscarried. He didn't want children. He knew that I did, so he had a vasectomy without telling me. He said…he said he only stayed married to me because I was a convenient excuse. Whenever one of his girlfriends pressured him for marriage, he could point to me and say I'd never give him a divorce." She paused and bowed her head, one hand on her pregnant belly. "I'd forgiven him so many times over the years, for so many indiscretions, but I couldn't forgive this. It was the final betrayal. I packed my things.

"I planned to come home and tell everyone I'd left Billy for good, but then he was killed. Everyone was so heartbroken. How could I tell you all we were on the verge of divorce, that Billy had been cheating on me for years?"

Lauren's face crumpled in tears. "I never wanted him to die, but I was so angry. In our last fight I told him I never wanted to see him again. I told him after everything he'd done to me, he was dead to me. And then he died on that highway."

"It's not your fault. It was an accident," Cole said.

"I kept thinking that maybe he'd been distracted by our fight. All it would take is one error—"

"It's not your fault," he said again, holding her close.

Ella lowered herself onto the sofa and wept. "I was so looking forward to the arrival of Billy's baby. It was like I'd still have a piece of my boy with me."

Grace Saunders put her arm around Ella's shoulders. "This baby is still your grandchild, Ella. You can celebrate that."

"You don't understand." She pulled a tissue from her pocket and blew her nose. "It's not the same."

"It's exactly the same," Lauren said, lifting her chin in a defiant angle. "This baby deserves your love. She shouldn't be thought of as inferior."

"But I've lost my son, and now I've lost his child."

"I'm sorry, Ella. I know you're grieving for Billy," Lauren said. "But you still have a son. He's right here, and he loves you. He's a good man, and he's going to be an amazing father. He deserves your respect. I won't tolerate you treating him or my daughter with anything less than your deepest love."

She closed her eyes, inhaling sharply and blowing her breath out through her mouth. Cole felt a shudder wrack her small frame.

"Lauren?"

"I love you, Cole. I'm so sorry I never told you before. I should have been shouting it from the rooftops. I'm sorry I listened to lies. Can you ever forgive me?"

Before he could answer, she groaned and doubled over, her hands going to her knees. "I think this might be a good time to take me to the hospital. The baby's coming."

Within five minutes they were in the back seat of Charlotte's Jeep, racing to the hospital. Charlotte drove while Garrett phoned the hospital in Bismarck between timing Lauren's contractions.

"Remember to breathe, sweetheart. The way we learned," Cole urged.

She ignored his instructions. "I'm sorry, Cole. Can you ever forgive me?"

"Baby, there's nothing to forgive. We both made mistakes, but it's over now. I'm so proud of you. You're the strongest, most courageous person I know. I love you."

"I love you, too."

She inhaled deeply as another contraction gripped her. Cole rubbed her back, trying to give her some relief. "Breathe through it, baby. You can do it."

"That's two minutes since the last contraction," Garrett announced. "You'd better step on it, Charlotte."

"Hang in there, Lauren. We'll be at the hospital in a few minutes," she said.

Cole massaged her shoulders. "Lauren, why didn't you tell your family you were in labor? They could have taken you to the hospital."

She shook her head, her breath coming out in little puffs. "I had to wait for you. I had to make things right before the baby came. And I want you there, in the delivery room with us. I want you to be the first person our daughter sees." She inhaled deeply. "I didn't want to lose you."

He kissed her forehead, emotion swamping him. "You could never lose me. We're in this thing together. Forever."

Epilogue

June 21

"Happy Father's Day to my two favorite dads."

Lauren set the cake on the dining room table in front of Cole and her father. Robert stuck two candles into the frosting and lit them.

Cole couldn't help but laugh. "I thought candles were for birthday cakes."

"Who says they can't be for Father's Day cakes too?" Lauren said with a grin. She hugged Cole's neck and kissed his cheek. "I wanted something special for your first Father's Day. And so did Piper, didn't you, sweetheart?"

Their almost-three-month-old daughter kicked her arms and legs at the sound of her mother's voice. Cole adjusted her in his arms and kissed the top of her downy head. Love for his child swamped him. Piper was the light and joy of his life. With her dark hair and green eyes, she was already a beautiful little replica of her mother. More importantly, she was healthy and strong.

And she was his. He didn't have to pretend she was another man's child. For that he was grateful every day for his wife's courage.

In addition to their families, he and Lauren had decided to tell their friends and co-workers the truth about Piper's parentage. They didn't want to pretend, and they didn't want Piper to be confused about who her father really was as she got older.

It hadn't been easy. He'd heard the gossip. As the news spread around town, there'd been speculation that he and Lauren had run around behind Billy's back for years. Billy had been such a hero in his hometown that many people took his side.

He didn't care. People would believe what they wanted to believe, and he couldn't change that. The people who loved and cared about them knew the truth and accepted it, and that was all that mattered.

"Okay, you two dads. Time to blow out the candles," Lauren said.

"Wait!" Charlotte said. "I want to get a picture." She grabbed her phone and snapped some photos. "I want to get some pictures of Piper later, too."

Lauren laughed. "You've taken more pictures of Piper than we have."

"Well, she is my favorite niece."

"Our only niece, you mean," Garrett said. "Speaking of only children, Lauren, you and Cole should have another baby. We need some boys in this family."

Lauren rolled her eyes at her brother. "Jeez, give us a couple of minutes, will you? Someday Piper will have a little brother or sister, but not for a while. I got my acceptance letter on Friday from the University of North Dakota in Bismarck. I'm starting back in September. It'll take me a couple of years, but I'll be able to finish my accounting degree."

"Honey, that's great news," Grace said. "I'm really proud of you."

"Thanks, Mom."

"Who's going to stay with the baby?" his mother asked.

"I got a place for her at the campus daycare, Ella. We'll be driving into Bismarck three days a week for my classes."

"Well, if my granddaughter decides she doesn't like daycare, she can stay with me, can't you, precious?"

Ella leaned in and tickled Piper's tummy. The baby made a gurgling sound in response, and her grandmother beamed at her. The change in Cole's mother in the last three months had been truly remarkable. One look at Piper and she'd been smitten. It didn't seem to matter to her anymore that she wasn't Billy's child. Ella would always mourn for Billy, and now that Cole had his own child, he understood how deep a parent's love for a child could be. But he'd never understand how she could have treated him so differently from his brother. If he and Lauren had another child, he'd be very careful to treat them equally. All the same, he was thrilled Ella loved his daughter without reservation.

"Ella, I'm sure we're going to need plenty of babysitting help in the next couple of years. Thank you."

His mother stroked Piper's hair. "That's what grandmas are for."

"I'm starved. I think it's time to cut the cake," Robert said, rubbing his hands together.

Lauren handed her father a knife and hugged him around the neck.

"Happy Father's Day, Dad. I love you," she said.

"I love you, too, sweetie. Thank you for the wonderful dinner. Nothing makes me happier than having my whole family together."

Lauren smiled at Cole and reached out her hand to him. "Nothing makes me happier either, Dad. I've got everything I need right here."

Cole brought her hand to his lips for a kiss. Their gazes locked in silent communion. She was absolutely right. Everything he needed was right here.

A word about the author…

Jana Richards has been making up stories since childhood, but she was in her thirties before she began to put pen to paper. While romantic suspense is one of her favorites, contemporary romance holds a special place in her heart. She loves writing romance fiction because of its message of hopefulness and its steadfast belief that love makes people better human beings.

When not writing or working at her day job as an office administrator, Jana can be found reading, gardening, spending time with her family, or tearing up her favorite golf course. Jana lives in Manitoba, Canada with her husband and daughters.

Visit Jana at http://www.janarichards.com

Thank you for purchasing
this publication of The Wild Rose Press, Inc.

For questions or more information
contact us at
info@thewildrosepress.com.

The Wild Rose Press, Inc.
www.thewildrosepress.com

To visit with authors of
The Wild Rose Press, Inc.
join our yahoo loop at
http://groups.yahoo.com/group/thewildrosepress/

www.ingramcontent.com/pod-product-compliance
Lightning Source LLC
La Vergne TN
LVHW050617100826
845148LV00011B/1619

* 9 7 8 1 5 0 9 2 2 4 8 0 7 *